PRAISE FOR IRIS MORLAND

Till There Was You

This is another lovely addition to this beautiful romantic series. I very much enjoyed this story, which was heartfelt and steamy. In particular, the growth of the main character as she finds her courage and independence is handled very well. The book does stand alone but the series is so good, you'll want to read them all!

— READER REVIEW

Someone to Watch Over Me

If you want a contemporary romance with family, reality and angst, love, bits of humor, hawt men and steamy love scenes...this is it.

— READER REVIEW

Dream a Little Dream of Me

Dream a Little Dream of Me was incredible. The chemistry between Lizzie and Trent was explosive.

If I Can't Have You

Richly heartwarming, sweetly emotional, undeniably sexy and very realistic small town romance. The details and descriptions given make for a fully engaging journey. Perfect summer sun in the backyard forgetting the world around you read.

The Very Thought of You

This might be my favorite of Morland's books thus far! The hate-to-love progression was well done and made for a compelling read. I couldn't put it down - read the whole thing in one day (and almost cried at one point)!

The Nearness of You

The trait I enjoy most in Iris Morland's work as an author is that she shows her characters as they are, not as they hope to be. That is what makes The Nearness of You so compelling.

THEN CAME YOU

THE YOUNGERS BOOK 1

IRIS MORLAND

BLUE VIOLET PRESS LLC

For my spice girls—rock on.

THEN CAME YOU

*V*iolet Fielding grimaced when her phone started ringing for what felt like the millionth time that day. She didn't need to look at the caller ID to know it was a creditor calling. Switching her phone to vibrate, she decided she'd earned a bit of denial time. If she didn't hear or sce the phonc calls, then they didn't exist, right?

Violet felt her desk vibrate with another phone call. Swearing under her breath, she turned her phone off and was halfway tempted to throw it out the window for good measure. Except she couldn't afford to buy a new phone just because she wanted to break her current one in a fit of pique.

Her desk was currently covered in beads, wires, charms, and crystals, all part of her jewelry business that she'd started four years prior. A necklace she had begun for one of her favorite clients sat on her desk, only half-finished, and it seemed to be judging her silently.

"Don't look at me like that," Violet muttered at the necklace. She pushed it aside. If she was talking to inanimate objects now, she definitely needed a break. Maybe a vacation far, far away. Did creditors exist in places like Siberia?

Violet blew out a breath. She was thirty-three, a widow, and she'd recently moved to the small town of Fair Haven, Washington. Violet had moved in with her mother-in-law, Martha Fielding, to help care for her, although Martha would adamantly deny that she needed any help. Even at sixty-six, she was a fiery woman who wasn't about to let anyone coddle her. Violet loved her for it and had thought of her as a second mother figure from the moment Violet's husband, William, gone two years now, had first introduced them.

"Violet, are you hungry?" Martha called from the hallway. "I'm starving. Do you want me to order takeout for dinner?"

Considering that Martha suffered from diabetes, she definitely didn't need to be eating pizza or Chinese.

"No, I'll make something," said Violet as she went to the kitchen. She opened the fridge, but despite the plethora of potential ingredients, her brain was too distracted to think of anything to make.

"Just not that kale soup," said Martha as she snagged a sparkling water from around Violet. Martha's soda addiction had had to end when her diabetes had worsened within the last two years. She'd given up sugary soda for diet soda, but Violet had persuaded her to try sparkling water instead. Martha had only agreed on the condition that Violet promise not to force her to eat tofu ever again.

"We don't have kale anyway."

Violet took out some chicken, some spinach, and a lemon, but when she realized ten minutes later that she'd forgotten to turn on the burner to boil the water for pasta, she uttered a few choice words.

Martha clucked her tongue at Violet's swearing. She was a wiry woman with bright silvery-blond hair and over-sized plastic glasses that she'd worn since the early 80s. She was barely five feet tall, but that didn't stop her from wearing ridiculously tall high heels. Always stylish, she continued to match her purse with her shoes and wore hats like she had in her youth. "People not wearing hats anymore is a travesty," she always bemoaned. "In my day, no woman went outside without one on."

"You seem distracted," Martha remarked as Violet began de-stemming the spinach. Martha made a face at the sparkling water she was attempting to drink but kept sipping it anyway. "Anything the matter?"

Considering that Violet had promised Martha she'd take care of her from now on, she wasn't about to tell her about how her jewelry business was collapsing in on itself, or how she owed more than she made. She'd thought that she'd be able to make things right, that it was just a brief hiccup. Now she wasn't so sure the ship could be kept from sinking.

"Nothing's wrong. When was the last time you tested your blood sugar?"

"Oh, don't fuss. I'm a grown woman. I'm fine. I keep telling you. All these tests and pills." Martha scoffed. "When I was a girl—"

"You used leeches and prayer when you were sick?" Violet smiled.

"Don't be rude to your elders." Martha took another sip of her water and frowned. "We definitely didn't drink schlock like *this*."

When Martha frowned like that, she reminded Violet of William. William had been the love of Violet's life. They'd met in college at the University of Washington. William had seemed an odd choice for Violet, a popular sorority girl who had wanted to go into fashion design. William had been bookish, an engineering major, but when they'd had to work on a group project for their ancient history class, he'd surprised Violet and asked her out. To everyone's shock, she'd said yes.

They'd gotten engaged right out of college and had been married a year later.

Only eight years after that, William had died one rainy night when his car had been T-boned. William had been killed instantly from the impact. Violet would never forget getting the call from the police officer that night, telling her there had been an accident and that her husband hadn't survived.

She pushed the memories aside. She could do that now, to some extent. The grief still lurked and took hold of her at times, but it wasn't as often as in the beginning. Sometimes Violet could even see a future for herself: one that no longer included William.

"What do you want to do tonight? Dominoes or checkers?" Violet asked as she and Martha ate dinner together.

Martha's eagle-eyed gaze made Violet want to squirm in her seat. "Why don't you go out for once? You don't need to stay in and entertain an old woman every night."

"I like entertaining old women."

"I think you use it as an excuse to avoid interacting with anyone your age. Especially anyone male." Martha's expression softened. "I know how much you loved my son. I miss him too, every day. But I knew the day that I lost my dear Harold that you can't stop living life when you lose people. Because then what's the point of living?"

Violet's throat closed. Was she avoiding living life, even two years later? It was true that she hadn't looked at a man since William's death. It would feel like a betrayal. She twisted her wedding ring, which she continued to wear every day, around her finger.

"I just moved here. Where would I go?"

"Oh, honey, it's a small town. Where else? Go to a bar. Get a drink. Meet a man. Maybe go home with him."

Violet almost choked on her water. "Martha!"

"Don't get your panties in a twist. I'm old, not dead. Nothing wrong with enjoying some male companionship. Why, I've been meaning to call up Dennis—"

Violet held up a hand, stifling wild laughter. "Please, no, I don't want to know."

"And your generation says *my* generation is prudish. You have to get out there. You're young. You could marry again. Don't hide behind William's death. I know it's hard to get back up into the saddle, but trust me: if anyone can do it, you can."

Violet peered more closely at Martha. "What's this all about suddenly?"

"Nothing." At Violet's skeptical look, she added, "Okay, maybe not nothing. There's a singles' meet-and-greet tonight—"

Violet groaned. "God, no, please. I've done those."

"You did one once a year ago and you stayed for fifteen minutes, or so you told me. You have to actually try." Martha pulled out a folded piece of paper and pushed it toward Violet.

"You should go."

"Martha—"

"No, don't. I appreciate everything you've done for me, how you moved here, how you help me. This is me helping you."

Violet smiled, feeling her eyes getting damp, and she squeezed Martha's hand in silent thanks. Before either of them could be reduced to tears, Violet changed the subject, deciding she'd much rather hear about Martha's male companion, Dennis, than think about William or her own mess of a life.

Violet didn't want to go to a singles' meet-and-greet, because if she met someone new, that would mean William was truly gone. It meant she had to open herself up to potential heartbreak all over again.

How could she fall in love when she'd already lost the love of her life?

But she also wanted to make Martha happy. So she put on her big girl panties (which were actually tiny panties that seemed more appropriate for meeting men), her newest top and a necklace she'd made for herself before applying bright red lipstick and a little mascara. After a brief hesitation, she took off her wedding ring. It was just for the night, she told herself. Glancing at herself in the mirror, she looked tired. At least bars were dark, and hopefully nobody would notice the bags under her eyes.

"Have a good time," said Martha, already happily ensconced in her favorite recliner, watching her soap operas she'd recorded earlier that day. "Don't forget to smile!"

Smile, yes. Men liked women who smiled. They didn't so much like women who cried when they heard songs that reminded them of their dead husbands, or who had creditors beating down their doors for money, or—

This will end well. Violet laughed under her breath. At least she'd hopefully get a free drink or two out of the bargain.

When she arrived at the bar called the Fainting Goat, she breathed in the scents of greasy food and booze while trying to steady her pounding heart. The bar was packed, and she couldn't tell if everyone was here for this singles' thing or if there were multiple parties here. She saw pink balloons in one part of the bar. When she got closer, she saw that one group seemed to be having a birthday party for a baby. Who had a party for a baby at a bar?

"Are you here for the singles' meet-and-greet?" a woman chirped before Violet could uncover the mystery behind the baby's bar birthday. "You look lost."

Violet laughed awkwardly. "Only a little. Is everyone here for this?"

"No, but we're the biggest group. Come sit with us and I'll introduce you. There aren't as many men here as I'd hoped. I'm Amber, by the way."

"Nice to meet you." Amber sat Violet down at a long table in the back where the meet-and-greet seemed to be happening. Although at the moment, it wasn't so much meeting and greeting as "avoiding eye contact and staring at your phone" instead.

"Hi there. I'm Violet." Violet held out her hand to the man to her right.

He muttered something under his breath at whatever he saw on his phone before looking up at her. "Hi, I'm Eddy. You go to things like this often? I can never find any women worth talking to."

Okay. "You know, I'm going to get a drink. Want anything?"

"I don't drink."

Rolling her eyes, she pushed through the crowd to the bar. If she was going to stay, she needed booze. The strongest they had, preferably.

"I'll have a gin and tonic," she told the bartender. "With extra gin."

The bartender was a man who seemed barely older than a high school student, yet his bartending skills were clearly those of a man who'd been in the business for years. Violet gave him an extra-large tip after he successfully tossed the bottle of gin into the air and caught it just as smoothly.

She drank her gin and tonic, savoring the coldness of the alcohol. People chatted and laughed all around her. She knew she should return to Amber and try talking to another single man, but she didn't have the heart for it. What was so wrong about being single? This wasn't Jane Austen: she wouldn't starve if she didn't find her own Mr. Darcy.

She turned and found herself with a perfect view of the birthday party. The baby, she realized, wasn't so much a baby as a toddler, and she seemed entranced by the giant pink birthday cake in front of her. A bunch of adults laughed when she tried to imitate the woman next to her by blowing out the candles—her mother, Violet presumed. A blond man with tattoos on his arms stood behind the toddler and helped her finish blowing out her second candle.

The adults all clapped and cheered. Another man with reddish-gold hair laughed, his teeth flashing in the dim light, when the toddler grabbed at her piece of cake with both hands and smeared her face with the pink frosting. The toddler squealed something that sounded like, "Cake!" in between pushing fistfuls of the cake and frosting into her mouth.

"Good one, Bea," the man said with a chuckle. "That's how to enjoy your birthday."

When the man turned toward her in profile, she couldn't help but find herself arrested by him. He had a square jaw, his nose aquiline, and she'd never seen hair quite that color. It was almost berry-colored, she thought. Her heart started pounding, especially when the man caught her staring and sent her a slow grin that she felt all the way to her toes.

She whirled around on her barstool and took such a deep drink of her gin and tonic that she started coughing. *How awkward!* Now that man would think she was a total weirdo who just stared at people for no reason.

"Can I get a glass of water?" she asked the bartender, her eyes watering.

As if he knew that her life was a mess, he looked sympathetic as he pushed a glass toward her. "Don't drink it too fast," he admonished.

I'm probably old enough to be your mother, she thought in irritation. Drinking the water, she dabbed at her eyes and hoped to God that the man hadn't seen her sputtering like a stopped-up chimney.

"What are you drinking? Gin and tonic?" Eddy slid in next to her and motioned at the bartender. "I've never liked gin and tonic. Bartender, can I get a Coke?"

The bartender rolled his eyes when Eddy wasn't looking, causing Violet to stifle laughter.

"Oh, no ice. Sorry. Hurts my teeth." Eddy pushed the

Coke back toward the bartender. "Are you having fun?" he asked Violet.

"Oh, loads."

"That's surprising. I never have fun at these things. They're always rather dull."

She had to bite her tongue in half from saying something snarky. When Eddy received his Coke sans ice and started drinking it through a tiny straw, though, she almost started choking from trying to hold back her laughter.

"Sorry, man, but this is my date," a rumbling voice said over Violet's shoulder. "Could you move?"

Eddy's mouth opened and closed like a fish, but when the man moved toward him with a determined look, Eddy scrambled down and scuttled away.

To Violet's surprise, the man she'd been staring at slid in next to her and grinned, a grin that surely had to be illegal in all fifty states.

"I'm Ash Younger," he said, smooth as silk. "How is it I've never seen a woman as beautiful as you here before?"

*a*sh waited for her to reply. Usually when he used a line like that, the women either blushed or tittered. Most did both. This woman, though, just raised a blond eyebrow and looked him up and down like he was some kind of cretin.

That made his smile grow wider.

"How many times have you said that to a woman at this very bar?" was her reply. "I'm curious."

"Not as many times as you think."

"So, at least fifty times? One hundred? Give me a ball-park estimate."

He tipped his head back and laughed. "I'm flattered that you assume I'm so prolific."

She sipped her drink. "Or desperate," she muttered.

At twenty-seven, Ash knew two things: that he liked

women, and that he liked to keep his relationships short, sweet, and with a lot of sex until they inevitably fizzled out. Sometimes the women wanted something more serious; sometimes they were just as uninterested in commitment as he was.

It was rare, however, that any heterosexual woman between the ages of twenty and forty-five ever considered his advances a nuisance. Ash wasn't stupid: he knew what he looked like. He knew how to seduce a woman with words and heated looks. He knew that confidence and a few compliments could take any man a long way.

"Lucky for you," he said as he waved to Reggie the bartender, "I'm never desperate. Now, are you going to tell me your name at least? Or will I have to make one up for you?"

"Oh dear, what names do you have in mind?"

He ordered his usual—a whiskey sour—and turned back to her. "I'm thinking Delilah. Or Jezebel."

"Subtle. How Biblical of you, too." She pushed her hair over her shoulder, exposing the pale and delectable curve of her neck. "What if I said it was Gertrude?"

"Then I'd call you Gertrude like the gentleman I am."

Her lips curved into a smile. Ash had been with many women, but there was something about this one that had intrigued him the moment he'd seen her staring at him.

He had thought this night would be like every other with his family and in-laws: crazy and loud. Tonight they celebrated his niece Bea's second birthday; she was his older brother Trent's daughter and the darling of the entire

Younger clan. She was definitely the cutest, that was for sure.

Ash loved his family, which included his older siblings, Trent and Thea, along with his younger siblings, Phin and Lucy. Since their parents were both dead now, they'd had to stick together. Until Trent had reunited with his former girlfriend Lizzie and had finally married her. He'd never gotten Lizzie out of his head. Ash hadn't been a fan of Lizzie for breaking his brother's heart, but at least they were all happy now. Sometimes they were so happy that it made Ash's teeth hurt.

Ash wasn't meant for marriage. He'd known that since he was a kid. He'd seen what marriage—and love—did to a person when he'd watched his own mother fall apart from his father's twisted type of love.

No, Ash didn't do love. But sex? Yes, he did that *very* well.

"My name's Violet."

"Violet." Ash couldn't help but notice that she was leaning closer to him now. "It suits you."

"I'm glad you think so, since it's the only name I have." She glanced over her shoulder. "It looks like your family is about to open presents. Is she yours?"

"Who? Bea? No, she's my niece. The first one in the family, so everyone spoils her rotten."

Violet smiled. "She's adorable. I can't blame you one bit." She shrugged a shoulder. "You should probably get back to the party."

"Are you trying to get rid of me?"

"I would never be so rude."

When she turned away from him, though, he got the message: he wasn't going to get anywhere with her. His own innate stubbornness made him want to stay and persuade her, coax her, make her laugh and blush. His more rational side, the same side that loved numbers, statistics, and algorithms, told him that he shouldn't hedge his bets. *Take this one as a loss. It happens to everyone.*

But it didn't happen to *him*. He was torn between amusement and annoyance and wasn't sure which emotion would win out.

"Ash, there you are," said his sister Thea as she same up to the bar. With her blond hair cut in a pixie and with a septum piercing, Thea looked like the lead singer of some rock band instead of a receptionist at a law office. "We're opening presents, and yours is next." Thea glanced at Violet with a raised eyebrow. "Although if you're busy—"

Violet was still focused on her drink and seemed to have forgotten all about him. *Ouch.* "No, I'm not busy."

Returning to the party, Ash drank his whiskey sour and got another as Bea ripped open her presents with undisguised glee. At two years old, she was more interested in the ribbons and wrapping paper than the toys and clothes. When Lizzie took a piece of ribbon from her that she was chewing on, Bea's face screwed up and went bright red before she let out a wail that practically made the walls of the restaurant shake.

"Here's your rabbit," said Lizzie as she picked Bea up from the high chair and gave her her favorite stuffed animal. "Hush, baby." She looked at Trent. "I think Bea's had enough for tonight."

Trent caressed Bea's cheek as she continued crying and rubbing her face in her mother's shoulder. Ash didn't know a damn thing about babies, but even he could tell when one was completely exhausted and overstimulated.

Lizzie soothed Bea, and eventually the toddler fell asleep in her mother's arms. Ash sat down next to Thea, across from whom sat Phin and Lucy. Phin worked as a lawyer in Portland, while Lucy was chasing her dreams of becoming an actress in Los Angeles.

Phin was the quiet brother who tended to avoid crowds, while Lucy was more like Ash, in that she lit up around people. She laughed and chatted with Abby and Megan Thornton, Lizzie's sisters-in-law. Lucy was tall yet lithe, her hair a dark auburn. With her wide gray eyes and sharp cheekbones, she had been approached to do modeling jobs more than once, but she'd always turned them down because she wanted to be an actress and nothing else.

"Having fun?" Ash asked Phin from across the table. "You look miserable, bro."

Phin's mouth twisted. "'Miserable' is a bit hyperbolic."

"Only you would use the word 'hyperbolic' in conversation."

"That's because Phin is the smartest of us all," said Thea without any envy. "He did graduate from high school early."

Phin didn't deny this assertion, because he knew very well that he was intelligent. Ash had always admired his younger brother's drive and focus. Ash had always been more of a will-o'-the-wisp in comparison. Hell, even Trent had settled down despite his aimless past: he'd since opened his three restaurants and now had a family.

Some days Ash didn't recognize the siblings he'd known growing up. *They've grown up*, his logical side said. *Maybe you should try it.*

He tipped back his drink and swiftly shoved that thought aside.

"Will you hold Bea for a second?" Lizzie asked Thea. "She's asleep, but I have to pee and Trent is making drinks—"

Thea was about to open her mouth when Ash interrupted. "I'll take her." At the women's looks, he rolled his eyes. "Guys, I've held her before."

"Yeah, but you don't usually volunteer," countered Thea.

"Don't be sexist," he joked as Lizzie gently handed Bea to him. The toddler murmured in her sleep before snuggling closer. She found her fist and began sucking her thumb, which Ash found beyond adorable but would never admit it.

"Hey, I'm all about men holding babies. They are fifty percent of the reason they happen," said Thea as she brushed a hand over Bea's dark curls. "She almost makes me want to have one of my own."

"Not me," said Lucy. "Babies put your life on hold."

"We know you're going to be a famous actress," said Ash, "and besides, you're what? Twenty-two?"

Lucy stuck out her tongue. "Twenty-three."

"So, a baby. I don't need my baby sister having a baby anytime soon." Ash shuddered. He still didn't like Lucy out in LA on her own, let alone the thought of some creep getting her pregnant.

Lucy's attention was eventually snagged elsewhere while Phin found himself cornered by James, Harrison and Sara Thornton's ten-year-old son. Harrison was Lizzie's eldest brother, and he and Sara had been married for three years now. Although James was her son from her previous marriage, Harrison had essentially adopted the boy as his own.

Bea cooed in her sleep, and Ash rested his chin on top of her head.

Thea said quietly, "Do you ever think about getting married? Having kids?"

Out of all of his siblings, Ash had always felt like Thea was the one most like him. Although she worked as a receptionist, her real passion was for art. Currently, she was working on a graphic novel. With her exuberance and tendency to be rather absentminded, Thea wasn't the least bit suited for an office job. Ash might be a pencil pusher who loved numbers and worked as Trent's accountant for his restaurants, but he still understood Thea's desire for freedom.

"No, I don't," he said without hesitation. "I've always known that life wasn't for me."

"Really? Because you already have a secret wife and kids you haven't told us about?"

"Because we've both seen the bad side of marriage. You saw how Mom was." He shuddered. "No, thanks."

Thea shrugged. "I get that, but we aren't our parents, either."

"So says the woman who hasn't dated seriously in how long?"

"There's no one worth dating around here. And you're one to talk."

He couldn't disagree. Thinking of dating, though, inevitably drew his gaze back to Violet, who now had a small group of women around her as she showed them what looked like pieces of jewelry.

Was she selling jewelry in a bar on a Friday night? He marveled at her. Where in God's name had she come from?

Thea looked over her shoulder. "Oh, she's still here. I saw you talking to her. She seems nice, so you should really leave her alone."

"We were just talking."

"Wait, don't tell me." Thea's eyes widened. "Did she turn you down?"

Ash just glared.

Thea laughed and clapped a hand over her mouth when Bea stirred. "No way! Oh my God, I love her already. What's her name? I'm going to marry her and I'm not even gay."

Ash rolled his eyes. "I've been turned down before."

"When? I want dates. I want times. I want the names and the exact words they used."

He and Thea bickered until Lizzie finally returned to

take Bea from him. After that, Ash watched Violet, completely mesmerized as she continued to show her wares.

She was clearly in her element. She helped one woman try on a necklace made of amber beads. When one of the other women said something, Violet laughed, her blue eyes sparkling.

Ash wanted to be the one who made her eyes sparkle. He wanted to make her laugh. And by God, he wanted to make her tremble as he kissed her.

Violet pulled out more jewelry from her purse. Did she keep her entire inventory in there? Considering how large the bag was, he could believe that she did. In a few more minutes, she'd given out her business card to at least half a dozen women and sold three pieces of jewelry, too. Amazing. He had to find out who she really was.

Once the women drifted away, Ash got up and slid into the chair next to Violet again. Currently, she was placing jewelry in individual plastic bags, completely unaware he'd returned.

"Do you have any jewelry for guys?" he asked.

She jumped. Clutching a plastic bag to her chest, she said, "You scared me!"

"My question still stands. Do you have anything for me?"

"Sadly, I'm out of bejeweled muzzles."

He leaned closer to her. "Oh, don't worry, sweetheart," he murmured, "I can still drive any woman wild, muzzled or not."

Finally, a slight blush crept up her cheeks. Ash wanted

to whoop in victory. Inhaling her floral scent, he felt his body stir, his blood pumping and desire flaring in his gut.

Violet huffed out a laugh. "If you're going to bug me, at least buy me a drink."

"It would be my pleasure."

3

*V*iolet knew that she should get up and leave. Ash was way too handsome and way too seductive for the likes of her. He practically oozed sensuality with his smile. She hadn't had sex since William had died. To be honest, she hadn't even thought about it—until this very moment.

With Ash looking at her with a very obvious *I want you* gaze and his hair falling across his forehead, his jawline like that of a Greek god? How did he *do* that? It wasn't fair. Violet wasn't stupid enough to think she could combat such raw sex appeal.

So, she did what she always did: she acted like nothing was happening.

She sipped her gin and tonic, amused that Ash had noticed what she'd been drinking and had ordered for her. She decided right then that if he was so intent on getting into her pants, he'd have to put in a lot of effort to get there.

Ash's lips quirked as he watched her sip her drink in silence. "You sell jewelry?"

"I make and sell it, yes. I have my own business."

"Really? When did you start it?"

Violet knew very well that most people didn't really care about the specifics when they asked questions: once she got into things like inventory and financial projections and clasps and chain types, their eyes glazed over, and she knew they'd heard nothing at all.

"I started it about four years ago. I was at a job that I hated, and I was tired of it. I was making jewelry in my spare time, and people started buying it, to my surprise. They wanted more. I was making enough that I was able to work on my business full-time soon after."

"Impressive. How did you start making your own jewelry?"

She wasn't at all certain that he really cared, but she shrugged inwardly. She'd tell him everything about bead sizes and charms and pliers and wire until he fell asleep at the bar.

"I took a class and I loved it. I ended up taking more classes, and it kind of snowballed from there." She opened her purse and brought out a number of samples that she'd already shown to the group of women, placing them in front of Ash. "I mostly make earrings, bracelets, and my favorite, necklaces. Rings, too. This necklace here? It's made with an infinity chain—see the figure eights?"

Ash leaned closer. "Oh yeah, I see it. I didn't know there were that many types of chains."

She bit back a chuckle, mostly because he was trying to sound enthused. *That's more than I can say for most people who don't care about jewelry*, she thought.

"It's one of my favorite types of chains. I wanted the chain to be fairly delicate with the larger beads and the flower that makes it a statement piece." She smiled kindly at Ash's slightly glazed expression. "Am I boring you?"

"Not at all." He held up a pair of chandelier earrings. "How did you put these together?"

Violet wondered what his game was. Suspicious and amused, she gave him an in-depth explanation about how she'd cut the wires, chosen the beads and beaded the earring. To her astonishment, not only did he stay focused on her as she talked, but he asked salient questions that showed he'd truly been listening.

I'm so doomed, she thought miserably. *Why couldn't he have been a jerk? Hot guys are always jerks!*

Ash just smiled and drank his whiskey sour without another word. His eyes seemed to challenge her, like he'd known she'd assumed he was just some self-centered douche and nothing else. *Fine, you won that round*, she thought, *but the game isn't over yet.*

"Enough about me, though," Violet said briskly, "tell me about you. What do you do?"

Ash leaned back on his barstool, his posture relaxed and open. "Nothing quite as exciting as jewelry. I'm an accountant for my brother's restaurants. Also his financial advisor. I take care of all of his books, more or less."

"Are the restaurants here in town?"

"I guess you wouldn't know, would you? This is one," he said as he pointed toward the ceiling. "Plus La Bonita and the Wishing Well."

She blinked. "Your brother owns all three?"

"Yes. My brother is Trent Younger, although I'm actually *younger* than him." He rolled his eyes at his pun and Violet laughed.

She hadn't heard anything about Ash's family, although in Fair Haven, the family that was most talked about was the Thorntons. They were the most prestigious—and wealthy— family living in the town, and Martha had told her all about the huge mansion in the hills where the parents still lived. They also had a bunch of children—five, six, seven? Something like that.

"Is it just you and your brother, then?" she asked.

He snorted. "I wish. I'm one of five."

"Wow, what is it with huge families around here? Is there something in the water?"

"Not much else to do in a small town except make babies, I guess," he said with a lazy, heated grin.

Violet felt a blush climb her cheeks, annoyed at herself for letting Ash get a rise out of her.

"I have a question for you," he said. "How is it someone as beautiful as you is single?"

"Because I'm actually an old, wrinkled crone underneath this mask."

He peered more closely at her. "If you are, it's a damn good mask. I can't even see your warts."

"You're hilarious."

"How old are you, then?"

She wrinkled her nose. "You can't ask a lady her age. You know better than that."

"I'm twenty-eight." At her dismayed expression, he added, "I promise I'm house-trained. I can even drive."

Violet instantly felt her age. It wasn't as if thirty-three was *old*, but five years' difference was enough to make her feel a bit like she was robbing the cradle. Besides, men tended to be less mature at twenty-eight than women were at that age. And how would Ash react when he found out how old she was? And that she'd been married and was now a widow?

She stirred her gin and tonic. "You're just a kid, then."

"You can't be more than..." Realizing he was heading into dangerous territory, he said, "Twenty-five."

"That was a close one. I'm thirty-three going on thirty-four this year, if you're dying to know. And now that I know how old you are, I'm absolutely sure you're way too young for me."

Setting his elbow on the counter, his expression amused, he said, "You don't even know me."

"I know enough about men."

"Do you? You don't strike me as the type who knows much about men at all."

She bristled. "My husband would disagree with that," she snapped.

Silence fell. Realizing what she'd said, she blushed in embarrassment, and when she reached to touch her wedding ring, her heart fell when she remembered she'd taken it off.

"You're married? You aren't wearing a ring." Ash frowned. "What are you doing at a singles' meet-and-greet, then?"

"Sorry, I'm not married anymore."

"Divorced?"

"Widowed."

Ash's face softened. "Sorry. How long ago...?"

She really, really didn't want to talk about William. It was like another betrayal in a way, talking to this man about her dead husband. Swallowing hard, she whispered, "Two years ago. Car accident. Please don't ask me anything else about him."

"Violet, I'm sorry."

He touched her hand, and she felt stupidly like crying. Taking a deep breath, she gave him a watery smile. "Sorry, I shouldn't have brought it up. Now, where were we? You were going to tell me all about how you balance your brother's books."

"I doubt you'd want an explanation about that. It's pretty dull stuff."

"Yet you seem to enjoy it."

He raised his eyebrows. "How could you tell?"

"Your voice. The look on your face. I wish I were good at numbers. I can make jewelry and sell it, but making the money make any sense is a challenge." When he looked like he wanted to ask more questions, she said, "No, no more serious stuff."

His voice got low, throaty, but then he said, "Tell me your favorite color."

She blinked. "Really? You didn't assume it's purple?"

"I'm not that predictable, and neither are you."

"You're right. It's green. Now, what's your favorite color? Gray like ash?"

They talked into the night, even when the woman from earlier came by to say something to Ash. Looking more closely at her, Violet realized that she must be one of his siblings. They both had the same eyes and hair color, and when the woman smiled, Violet saw Ash in that smile. It was almost eerie.

"We're all heading out," the woman said. "You coming?"

"No, I'm staying here for now."

The woman glanced at Violet, glanced back at Ash, then shrugged. Addressing Violet now, she said, "Make sure he behaves himself."

Ash rolled his eyes at her departure. "My older sister Thea. She's a pain in the ass."

"I just have one older sister. You're lucky to come from such a large family."

"That's one way to put it," he said wryly.

As the bar quieted somewhat, Ash moved closer to her, like a glacier slowly sliding downhill. And to Violet's dismay, she didn't want him to move away. He smelled so good— like wood smoke and spice—and his muscles bulged with each small movement. When he licked his lips after finishing his drink, her heart almost burst from her chest.

Danger, danger. Get out of here or you'll do something stupid. Like kiss him.

"What time is it? Oh, I need to get home. I need to feed my—" She racked her brain for an animal to feed and finally landed on, "Clown fish. My clown fish." *Clown fish, seriously?*

"Your clown fish. He needs to be fed at one sixteen a.m.?" Ash's lips twitched.

"Yes, he's a very particular fish. I got him when he was a baby fish and he's very important to me."

Violet paid for her drinks—not looking at Ash when she did it—returned her jewelry to her purse and practically sprinted out of the bar.

ASH WATCHED as Violet jogged down the sidewalk away from him. What the hell had he said or done to freak her out like that? He knew very well she didn't have to go feed a clown fish or whatever it was.

If she were simply uninterested in him, he'd let her be. But he'd seen the interest in her eyes, the way her pupils had dilated, the way she'd crossed her legs toward him. She'd played with her hair, she'd licked her lips. She'd had so many obvious tells that had screamed KISS ME, TAKE ME, that he'd had to restrain himself from kissing her right then and there in the bar.

"Violet, wait up," he said as he caught up to her. "Hey, talk to me." He touched her arm, and she stopped walking but didn't turn to look at him. "Look, if I said something that offended you, I apologize. Let me make it up to you."

She inhaled deeply before letting out a deep sigh. Her breath puffed white into the cold air. "You didn't do anything. Really." She finally looked at him. "Am I allowed to say 'it isn't you, it's me'?"

"That's almost as big of a lie as your fish."

She gasped, then laughed. "Excuse you, Marty the fish is very real and very important to me."

"Marty? Now I really know you're lying." He lowered his voice, wanting to sound inviting. Tempting. "Come on. I want to show you something."

Her blond eyebrows shot straight to her hairline. "Is that a euphemism?"

So much for tempting her. "No, it's not."

At this point, they'd moved toward the opening of an alleyway that afforded them some measure of privacy. The streetlights were just bright enough that Ash could make out Violet's expression somewhat, but she was still rendered rather shadowy. The mystery of her only intrigued him more. Who was she, really? And why did he want to know so badly?

"When's the last time you let yourself have any fun?" he asked.

His voice was a murmur, and he leaned down so he was almost touching her ear. To his delight, she was tall enough that he didn't have to lean far. He was used to getting a crick in his neck when kissing women. The thought of avoiding that small annoyance only added fuel to the fire of his desire for her.

"I have fun all the time," Violet countered.

"Name an example within the last week."

"I played dominoes with my mother-in-law." She said it with such verve that God almighty, he wanted to kiss her right then and there just so she could add some real fun to that pathetic list.

"No, I mean something fun with a person your age." He moved closer until her soft hair tickled his cheek. "When's the last time you let yourself have fun without worrying about the consequences?"

"I'm too old to do things like that."

Ash laughed softly. "You act like you already have one foot in the grave, when in fact you're a gorgeous, intelligent, *young* woman. Damn shame, in my opinion."

Violet huffed. "I didn't ask for your opinion about my life. And what about you? What kind of a guy picks up a woman during his niece's birthday party?"

"A man who knows what he wants."

"Oh my God, you're so, so——" She growled in frustration. "Annoying. Has anyone ever told you how annoying you are?"

He couldn't stop smiling; his face hurt from it. The rarity of a woman like Violet, who loved to banter and who didn't simper, was refreshing. Arousing.

"I'm never annoying to anyone," he said. "Now, you know what we're going to go do?"

"Work on our taxes?" She said it almost hopefully.

He touched the tip of her nose. "We're going to go have some fun and not worry about anyone else."

She hesitated: he could feel it in the way her body tensed. "I'm not going to sleep with you," she said in an anxious rush. "I don't know you, it's too soon—"

He pressed her lips together with his fingers, effectively cutting her off. "I'm not talking about sex." *At least not yet.* "I'm talking good, clean, wholesome fun."

She moved his hand away from her mouth. "With *you*?"

"Yes, me." Ash stepped away and held out his hand. "Do you trust me, Violet?"

She didn't move for a long moment. Right then, all he wanted was for her to say yes. Not just for his own enjoyment, but for hers, too.

It felt like an eternity before she said, "Yes, I trust you," and she placed her hand in his.

4

*V*iolet couldn't imagine where Ash wanted to take her at one thirty in the morning that *wasn't* to his place. When she said that she trusted him, her boring, logical side yelled, *You don't know him! Go home! You're crazy!*

And yet...her intuition told her she could trust him. She trusted that when he said he wanted to have "good, clean, wholesome fun," he meant it. At least, as much as Ash Younger could do anything wholesome.

She followed Ash down the street and out of the small downtown area. Tipping her head back, she could make out a few stars, and she felt like they were the only two people in the entire world. The town was so quiet. The only sounds were a dog barking and a single car driving by.

When they arrived at the playground, Violet let out a startled laugh. "This is what you had in mind?"

"What, do you have something against swings?" Ash sat

down in one of the swings that was so low to the ground—especially considering that he had to be over six feet tall—that Violet started giggling so hard that her stomach hurt.

She sat down next to him in a swing and started pumping her legs. At five-ten, she had to bend her legs until her heels touched her butt just to avoid scraping her feet against the sand below.

Ash swung next to her. When she glanced over at him, he sent her a brilliant smile. She shook her head.

"I can't imagine you went to a bar to pick up a woman just to take her to a playground."

"I like to think I'm not as obvious as you'd like to think," he countered.

Violet pumped her legs until she swung high into the air. She let out a deep sigh as she caught sight of the houses that sat in the hills overlooking Fair Haven. Lights twinkled from a few windows. She didn't mind that it was chilly outside or that her hands were freezing from the metal chains.

"Once when I was in first grade," said Ash as they swung higher and higher, "I tried to get into one of those baby swings. You know, the ones that look like a rubber diaper?"

Violet's lips twitched. "And?"

"Well, I was already big for my age, and hardly baby-sized. I managed to somehow get my legs into the leg holes and tried to swing, but soon realized that I'd made a very, very bad decision."

"Got a little bruised?"

He laughed. "My balls were sore for a week. When I tried to get out, I couldn't. I was stuck in a baby swing. My teacher had to call the fire department to cut me out."

Violet started laughing so hard that she lost her momentum. Gasping for breath, she wiped her eyes and was almost finished laughing before another bout of giggles burst from her.

"I'm glad you think my pain and anguish are so funny." Ash kept swinging next to her.

Suddenly emboldened, Violet began swinging again until they were neck and neck. "Whoever jumps the furthest wins a prize," she said.

"What, a broken arm?"

"Chicken."

He snorted. "Fine, it's a deal. What do you want?"

She considered. "If I win, you have to ride that dragon thing over there," she said as she pointed to the plastic dragon on a spring. "And I get to record it."

"Kinky." Ash swung down and then up again. "If I win," he said, his voice like dark velvet, "I get to kiss you."

Laughing breathlessly, she began to count down. On three, they jumped from their respective swings and landed on the sand below. Violet felt the air whoosh from her lungs, and Ash grunted as he landed with a loud thump.

Both gasping for air, Violet turned toward Ash, only to see him smiling like the cat that had caught the canary. His right arm stretched above his head, and when Violet did the same, she realized he'd technically jumped the furthest.

"No fair," she muttered, "your arms are longer than mine."

"All's fair in love and war."

He cupped her cheek, and everything else faded away as he brushed his mouth against hers. Violet's heart fluttered like a caught butterfly. He kissed her softly, playing with her bottom lip, his touch gentle. Violet melted against him, his body warm and solid. When she wrapped her arms around his neck, he growled and deepened the kiss until she saw stars under her eyelids.

She didn't care that it was the middle of the night, or that they were lying in the sand on a playground. She didn't care that she barely knew this man who kissed like the devil but who had the smile of an angel. Pressing closer to him, she tangled her tongue with his, loving the way he shuddered under her hands.

The kiss transformed into a conflagration, and before Violet knew it, she was under Ash as his hands roved all along her torso. She arched under his touch with abandon. Her inhibitions melted away with every stroke of his tongue and every caress of his hands.

"God, you're sweet," he muttered as he kissed down her throat, laving her collarbone. "I want you."

She knew he wanted her—she could feel his erection against her hip. And just as suddenly as the conflagration had begun, her rational mind emerged to ask her, *What are you doing?*

What was she doing? This wasn't her. She didn't do one-night stands. She didn't kiss strange men in parks.

Have you forgotten me already? William's voice resounded in her mind.

"I—no. Wait. Please stop." Her voice was shaky. "Stop."

Ash stopped, his forehead creased with concern. "What is it?"

Violet pushed at his arm, and he moved away enough that she could sit up. She took a deep breath.

"Sorry, it was just—a lot."

"Don't apologize. I let it get out of hand." He stood up and offered her a hand. "Do you want me to take you home?"

For some reason, she didn't want to go home because then this magical night—even with its random bumps and awkwardness—would end. Violet would have to return to being boring Violet Fielding, widow, failing entrepreneur, and a woman who was apparently too terrified to enjoy life or kiss a man in the park.

"No, I want to keep having fun." She pulled on his hand. "Let's go down the slide."

Ash seemed surprised, but he didn't comment on her strange behavior. He probably thought she was a bit of a loon. One minute she was cold, then hot, then cold. She couldn't understand her own behavior, either. So for the moment, she decided not to think about it.

Violet was good at a lot of things, but she excelled at denying what she didn't want to see.

That was the funny thing about denial: you could always deny that it even existed.

Ash had thought of going to the playground totally by chance. When he'd said that he'd wanted to show Violet something, he'd honestly had no idea what he'd even meant. What was open in the middle of the night that wasn't just another bar?

That random idea had turned into one of the best nights of his life—regardless of his skinned palm and newly bruised elbow.

"Ready?" He clambered onto the slide behind Violet and wrapped his arms around her waist. "Go!"

She squealed as they went down the slide before falling into a heap at the bottom. He laughed as she laughed, and all he wanted to do was kiss her again.

The streetlights surrounding the park provided enough illumination that he could make out her expression. She seemed relaxed for the first time that evening. Who would've thought he'd just needed to take her to the playground?

Getting up, he groaned a little. "I'm way too old for this," he muttered. He limped behind Violet to make her laugh again.

"Aren't I the old one here? Come on. You still haven't ridden that dragon thing."

"I distinctly remember something about you *losing* that bet."

"I'll ride one, too."

She looked at him over her shoulder, her hair blowing

in the night breeze, and it took every ounce of his self-control not to kiss her a second time.

That kiss, though. It had rocked his world. He'd had his fair share of amazing kisses, but that one had been something different. He almost didn't want to think too much about why that was.

As they sat on their respective springy animals, Ash didn't try to force past the silence that had fallen between them. He watched Violet instead: the way she pushed her hair over her shoulder, or how she tilted her head back to look up at the stars. In profile, she was somehow more beautiful, her nose a lovely angle that led to her pillowy lips, her right ear a whorl like a pale seashell.

"How long have you lived here?" she asked him.

"All my life, except for when I went to college. What about you?"

"I grew up in Yakima, went to UW. I was living in Bothell up until two weeks ago."

"So that's why I haven't seen you around here before."

"My mother-in-law needed help. She'd never admit it, but I knew she did."

He blinked in surprise. Weren't mothers-in-law always the type of people you stayed far away from? He'd never had one of his own, but considering how Trent's mother-in-law terrified all she knew, it hadn't seemed so much a stereotype as something that was true.

"You left everything behind for your mother in law?" He whistled. "I'm impressed. That's very nice of you."

"Martha has been like a mother to me since I first met

her. She was always so lovely to me, and especially after I married her son. I got lucky."

"What about your own mom?"

"She's busy traveling the country with my dad in their fancy new RV."

He laughed while at the same time envy stung him. He'd never had any kind of a mother—or father—figure in his life. His own mother had committed suicide when he'd been just a kid, and his father had died without any of his kids mourning his loss. Edward Younger had been mean, selfish, and a giant pain in the ass until his very last breath. He couldn't imagine moving to some tiny town like Fair Haven for someone not even his blood relative.

"How did you get into accounting?" she asked.

"I didn't know what else to major in." At her laughter, he shrugged. "It's true. I was always good at math, but science bored me. I needed to do something practical. I'm not a theater guy or musician or anything like that. I got my degree, messed around doing nothing for a bit until my brother hired me to do his books. My brother is annoying, but he's a good boss."

"You never had some dream job you wanted to do as a kid?"

His mouth twisted. "Not really. When you grow up poor and with shitty parents, your dream is mostly to get out of there as fast as you can. It's pretty much a miracle I got into college at all."

At her sad expression, he wanted to slap himself. *Nothing like a pity party to get a woman into your bed. Good job, dumbass.*

"I'm tired of talking, though." Getting up from his dragon ride, he held out his hand to Violet. She took it this time without hesitation. "Dance with me."

Violet bit back a smile as he led her into the grass surrounding the playground. Placing his hand on her trim waist, he allowed himself a moment of weakness to inhale her sweet scent, to feel her body against his own. They moved slowly, no music to be heard except the pounding of their hearts. When he twirled her around, she laughed breathlessly.

"Ash," she murmured, gazing up at him. "About that kiss earlier—"

"I won't kiss you again. Don't worry."

"No, I mean, don't apologize. I'm not sorry it happened. I just haven't done this in a long time. Not since before I met William."

Hearing her dead husband's name made him pull her closer, like he could keep her all to himself. What kind of person got jealous of a dead man? Apparently Ash did.

"Tonight has been lovely. I never thought I could have fun like that again," she admitted.

"I'm glad."

They danced in silence for a few moments longer until they stopped. Ash didn't let her go, and to his relief, she didn't back away. He watched her chest rise and fall, her breath puffing white in the cold air. If he were a gentleman, he'd take her home out of the cold.

But Ash had never been a gentleman, and he wasn't about to start now.

"Violet," he whispered. He touched her cheek. "I lied earlier."

She blinked. "What?"

"I lied about saying I wouldn't kiss you again. I want to kiss you again, right now, but I won't, unless you want me to."

She didn't reply for so long he thought he'd messed everything up again. Then, she curled her hand around the back of his neck and brought his mouth down to hers.

The second their lips touched, it was like a match lit. The first kiss had been about discovery; this kiss was all about fanning the flames of this passion that had come out of nowhere.

He kissed her hard, wrapping her in his arms, fireworks bursting in his skull. His cock hardened again, and when he rubbed against her, she gasped into his mouth.

"Come home with me," he said. He knew it sounded like a plea, but he didn't care. He needed her; he wanted her so badly it was like he'd die if she didn't say yes. "Come home with me. I'll make it so good for you."

Violet looked into his eyes. She caressed his jaw, and he felt that soft touch all the way to his toes.

"Come home with me," he said one last time.

She nodded. Then, "Yes."

It was a whisper, barely heard, but that was all he needed.

*a*sh opened the door to his apartment and waited for Violet to follow him inside. She didn't hesitate this time. Maybe in the morning, in the light of day, she'd regret what she was about to do. Maybe months, years, decades from now, she'd look back and say, "I should've stayed home. I should've done the safe thing."

She had a feeling the only regret she would have was if she didn't embrace this chance to be with a man like Ash.

"Okay?" Ash asked as he shut the door behind her. "You seem far away."

"I'm just amazed at how clean your apartment is for a single guy."

He snorted. "Haven't I told you? I'm house-trained and everything."

"And you own a vacuum? My hero."

When he growled and started tickling her, she gasped

between laughter. Only moments later, his hands held her still at her waist, his gaze no longer playful. It was intense, heated.

Licking her lips, she waited.

"I want you in my bed," he said, and his words were like a seductive spell surrounding her.

"I want that, too."

He took her hand and led her to the bedroom in the back of the apartment. He turned on a dim lamp in the corner, illuminating a bed covered in a navy-blue bedspread, books scattered on the bedside table. The room was clean, but rather bare, like Ash had only moved in recently.

The room's decor faded away when Ash dipped a finger into her cleavage, tugging on her blouse. "I want you naked."

She blushed, but only a little. She wanted that too. She wanted to feel him pressed against her, his warmth and his strength covering her. It was like a fever in her blood, this overwhelming *want*.

Violet hadn't had sex in years, and she'd had a fleeting fear that she'd forgotten how to do it. To her immense gratitude, she realized it was rather like riding a bike: you never really forgot.

She began to unbutton her blouse, and Ash's eyes darkened. She pushed the blouse off her arms, absurdly glad she'd worn the sexier bra and panties this evening. Normally she wore boring white; this lingerie set had been collecting dust in the back of her drawer for years.

"You're gorgeous." Ash touched her collarbone before cupping one of her breasts. He thumbed her nipple through the lace.

Although she wanted him to touch her everywhere, she didn't want this to be all about her. Pushing his hands away with a smile, she shook her head. "Your turn. I want to see you too."

He flashed her a grin. "Impatient?" Ash pulled his shirt over his head without any protest, revealing his toned abdomen.

Violet let out a sigh of appreciation. Trailing her hand from his sternum to his belly button, she marveled at how hot his skin was and how his muscles flexed and bulged with each breath he took. His ribs expanded as she brushed the tips of her finger near the bone of his pelvis. She could see the bulge in his jeans, and the knowledge that this man wanted her only emboldened her further.

Violet had always enjoyed sex. William had been a kind lover, although he'd never been particularly adventurous. They had tended to have sex at the same time on the same days, unless William had to go on a work trip. Then they'd move the sex to when he'd returned.

Violet realized now how very *boring* that had been. She whispered a silent apology to William for the thought, but it was true. She couldn't remember the last time she'd been this excited, like she could taste the anticipation on her tongue. Was it just the novelty of this situation? Or was it something about Ash himself?

She rubbed at a freckle on his hip before beginning to unbuckle his belt. "I want to see all of you," she whispered.

A slight flush had darkened his cheekbones. "I'm not going to stop you."

Violet's hands shook a little as she dipped her hand inside his boxers and cupped his length. Engorged already, his cock was bigger than she'd thought, and her heart tripped a little when she saw him completely.

He was gorgeous. She'd never thought that word in regard to a man, but it was true. Ash's breaths came faster as she squeezed his cock, his eyes hooded. She stroked him in slow movements, loving how she could torment a man like him with just a simple touch.

"A little firmer—yes, like that." He grunted when she rubbed the tip of his cock as a pearl of fluid emerged. "Shit, I haven't had a hand job like this in years."

She laughed. "I haven't given one in years, either."

"Clearly you're a master at it."

She felt clumsy and out of practice, but that didn't stop her from stroking him, faster and faster. When he blew out a long breath, a moment later his body tensed and he came, his seed splashing onto her hand.

"Damn. I should've had you stop, but I didn't want you to." He shook his head and then kissed her, and she moaned. "I'll be right back," he said as he broke the kiss and stepped away.

He soon returned with a washcloth. After she'd cleaned up, she found herself being pushed toward the bed. She landed with a bounce as Ash kneeled in front of her.

"We're not done?" Violet joked as Ash took off her boots.

"Do you want to be done?" He quirked an eyebrow.

"Hell, no." She unbuttoned her jeans and a shiver went through her at Ash's chuckle.

Soon, she was in just her panties and bra, sitting at the edge of the bed with Ash between her legs. Running her fingers through his hair, she tipped his head back and kissed him.

He kissed like he had all the time in the world, and Violet realized that she'd missed kissing a man more than she'd ever thought possible. She missed the taste, the way stubble rubbed at her chin. She'd just missed being with someone else.

"I didn't know guys liked to kiss like you do," she admitted.

"Men don't understand how important kissing can be. Besides, I like my women desperate for me by the time I slide inside them." He said the erotic words as he kissed and licked her throat before burying his face between her breasts. "If the woman isn't into it, it's not going to be good for me, either."

"How noble of you." Her words were breathy as Ash reached inside the cup of her bra and thumbed her nipple.

Memories of William tried to intrude right then, like her mind wanted to remind her that she was having sex with someone other than the love of her life. Would William be happy for her, doing something so out of character as sleeping with a man she'd just met? She didn't know. She wasn't sure if she wanted to know.

"How do you like it, Violet? Do you like it slow and steady until you come, or do you like it hard and fast until you're clawing your lover's arms and screaming his name?"

She inhaled. "I don't know. I mean, both sound lovely."

"Hmm, if that's the case..."

Ash reached behind her and unhooked her bra, and she helped him remove it. Her breasts ached, her nipples hardened nubs already, and when Ash palmed one breast, she shuddered.

She didn't have breasts of a twenty-year-old girl: she knew that very well. They were average-sized, neither so big as to get in the way nor so small as to force her to wear push-up bras. But as Ash gazed at her breasts, she felt like they were the most gorgeous set in existence.

"It's a shame you have to cover these beauties up." He licked the underside of one breast.

"I think I might get arrested if I didn't."

"Still. Tits this beautiful should be worshiped."

Violet had never in her life referred to her breasts in that way, but the vulgarity only sent a frisson of heat through her. Ash kissed and sucked her breasts and watched her every reaction, seeming to revel in each moan that emerged from her throat.

"I like slow and steady," she blurted. She whimpered when he nipped at the sensitive skin below her breasts. "Very slow and steady."

"Good thing we have all night. And all morning, if need be. I don't have to go into work until eleven."

"What a nice boss you have."

He snorted. "It helps that he has a toddler who likes to keep him and his wife up at night when she's teething, so he comes in later than me sometimes."

He kissed down her belly and hooked his fingers under the waistband of her panties before pulling them off completely. Now totally nude, Violet had to restrain herself from throwing a blanket over herself. She wasn't a prude, by any means, but she'd never had a man look at her so avidly when she had not a stitch of clothing on.

She'd put on some weight in the last year, her belly curving and hips flaring out more than when she was younger. She hadn't thought about waxing or shaving and she wondered if Ash would say something, and embarrassment flooded her when he gently parted her legs.

But she shouldn't have worried. His nostrils flared, his gaze growing darker, and when she touched the back of his neck, he shuddered, a full body shiver. He was hard again, his cock ruddy and long against his toned stomach.

Ash hooked his arms under her knees and placed her feet on his shoulders. Now completely open to him, she lay on the bed and closed her eyes; it was almost too much to feel *and* see everything going on.

She felt Ash's warm breath on the insides of her thighs, and then his mouth was on her sex. She gasped as his tongue traced her folds, the heat blooming inside her belly with every long, leisurely lick. She quivered and had to grab handfuls of the bedspread to hold on.

Ash groaned and muttered, his fingers digging into her thighs as he held her captive. Violet's eyes flew open when he mouthed her clit, and as he built and built her own pleasure, she felt like she wouldn't survive the impact. How could she? She'd never experienced such pure ecstasy, her every nerve singing with it.

He tongued her clit in relentless strokes, and in one last burst of pleasure, she came so hard that her quivering shook the bed. Ash kissed the insides of her thighs, his stubble a sharp contrast to the softness of his lips.

"Goddamn, Violet," he said as he stood up and undressed completely, "you're amazing. You know that, right?"

"I think my bones have melted."

He laughed. "That's a good sign." Going to the bedside table, he got out a condom and put it on before returning to the bed. He lay on his side, Violet having rolled to face him. She hitched her leg over his hip, opening herself once more to him. When his cock pressed against her still-sensitive center, they both groaned at the same time.

"I need to be inside you. You're killing me," he said.

She nodded, and then he was pushing inside her, the feeling glorious and almost too much. He was big, and she had to adjust to his size. But Ash went slow, watching her face.

Violet started undulating, needing that friction. She'd never been one to orgasm a second time in bed, but already, she could feel another one building. Ash thrust into her and began to move in a rhythm that made her wild. Her belly clenched, her breasts ached, and when Ash kissed her, she could only dig her nails into his arms and hang on.

He pounded into her. *So much for slow and steady*, she thought wildly. The sounds of their bodies slapping, the smell of sex and salt, the way Ash muttered her name under his breath like a prayer—everything coalesced and her second orgasm hit her with all of the subtlety of a freight train. She bit her lip to keep from screaming, her entire body shuddering.

"There you go, baby. God, you're amazing." Ash thrust a couple more times before she felt him coming, too, his cock pulsating inside her.

Violet was so boneless, so sated, that she barely remembered Ash disposing of the condom and turning off the light. Before she knew it, she succumbed to sleep and didn't stir until morning.

ASH AWOKE to the sound of a door closing. Sitting up with a lurch, it took him only a second to remember: Violet. Meeting her at the Fainting Goat, the playground. The sex. *Oh Christ, the sex.* The best sex of his life and instead of seeing her lying sleeping next to him the following morning, he saw nothing but a bracelet sitting on the pillow where she should've been lying.

Had a woman just up and left him without saying

goodbye after sleeping with him? That was a first. Usually he was the one tiptoeing out of a woman's house so as to avoid any awkward morning conversations.

He rubbed his eyes and groaned, glancing at the clock. He still had time to get into work on time. The last thing he needed was Trent grilling him about being late after Bea's birthday party last night. Most likely everyone had noticed that Ash had abandoned the party in favor of a beautiful woman.

He picked up the bracelet on the pillow, shaking his head a little. It was a simple bracelet made of twine and small orange-and-black-striped stones. There was a small handwritten note under the bracelet that read: *Tiger's eye for good luck and focus. —Violet.*

Good luck and focus? Was that what she'd gotten out of all of this? And had she made this bracelet while he'd been sleeping or had she already had it on hand? He could almost see her making the damn thing as he snored away, placing it on her pillow and sneaking out like a thief in the night. Or in this case, a thief in the morning.

As Ash got ready for work, he couldn't shake the feeling of being...used? He didn't know what word he was looking for. Maybe he had expected the usual female kind of reaction from Violet: cuddling in the morning, suggestions of seeing each other again. That glassy-eyed look of infatuation that many women wore after they'd slept with Ash. It wasn't love: just the aftermath of good sex with a side of infatuation.

Yet Violet hadn't even said goodbye. Did that mean she

hadn't enjoyed the sex? He shook his head. He knew she had: he'd felt her orgasm—twice, he thought with pride. She'd enjoyed it just as much as he had.

He tried to put the bracelet on before he left for work before realizing that it was too small. He smiled sadly as he turned it in the light to see how the beads shone.

Tiger's eye for good luck and focus. Well, he'd have a hell of a time focusing on anything today after last night. And for some reason, that thought unsettled him more than anything else.

6

*V*iolet stepped up to the brightly colored 1920s bungalow where Lizzie and Trent Younger lived and wondered if she'd lost her ever-loving mind.

He's not going to come over for a jewelry party. There's no way. Just act cool, Violet.

Easier said than done.

After she took a deep breath, she approached the front door and didn't even get to knock before Lizzie opened it with a wide smile, Bea on her hip.

"I saw you walking up. Oh, Trent, can you take Violet's things and put them in the living room? I would, but this one here doesn't want me to put her down today," she added as she looked pointedly at Bea. Right then, Bea had her fist in her mouth and seemed more than content to watch the proceedings.

Trent took Violet's boxes of jewelry, and the women followed him into the living room.

"I told him he had to make himself scarce," said Lizzie in a whisper, "and he's grumpy he doesn't get to watch the game on his new TV."

"I just bought it!" he said over his shoulder, grumbling.

"I told you that you could go to Megan and Caleb's, or Ash's place. They have big TVs."

"Not the same thing."

Violet shivered at the sound of Ash's name, her heartbeat picking up just at the mere mention of him.

It'd been a month since that night she'd spent with him. When she'd arrived home at the crack of dawn, she'd known that she'd made a huge mistake.

It wasn't that the sex had been bad. In fact, it had been amazing. Mind-blowing. It had shown Violet everything she'd been missing—and she didn't need that right now in her life. Besides, what kind of a relationship could she have with a playboy like Ash? He'd probably already moved on to his next conquest by now. She doubted he had to go without a woman in his bed for very long.

The thought of him with someone else made her stomach clench. She didn't want to think about that. Pushing the thought aside, she forced a smile on her face as the guests began to arrive.

When Lizzie had contacted Violet about hosting a party where Violet could sell her jewelry, Violet had had no reason to decline, no matter who Lizzie's brother-in-law was. It would've been the height of stupidity, especially considering that Lizzie was a well-known singer who was going to go on tour later in the year. If Lizzie wore just one of Violet's pieces at a show, it could be huge for Violet's business. It could be enough of a push to get her out of the hole that she'd dug while trying to get out of debt.

Lizzie's house was warm and inviting, the decor a mixture of bright colors and more muted neutrals. The living room where the party would be held was decorated with sleek furniture in shades of gray, with canary-yellow accents dotting the room.

Lizzie introduced Violet to a few women Violet had seen around Fair Haven, not realizing they were related to Lizzie somehow. Considering the size of the Thornton family, of which Lizzie was a member, it shouldn't have surprised Violet to find that so many people were connected —or outright married—to one of the members of that family.

Sara, Megan, and Abby were each married to a Thornton brother (Harrison, Caleb, and Mark, respectively). Rose DiMarco was engaged to Seth Thornton, and they were marrying in the summer. Thea Younger also came, and she reminded Violet so much of Ash that it hurt to hear her laugh and joke.

"Looks like everyone is here," said Lizzie as she sat on the couch next to Violet, Bea on her lap. "Let's get started. First of all, thank you so much for doing this, Violet. When I heard about your jewelry from Megan, I had to find out more, and when I realized that you make everything too, well, that sealed it."

"Don't let her buy everything," Trent called from the kitchen, "because that woman lives for jewelry."

"You just spent three grand on a TV!" Lizzie rolled her eyes, although Violet could tell the couple enjoyed teasing each other.

"What is it with men and TVs? It's like the bigger the screen, the more of a zombie they turn into," said Megan. With her red hair and pretty smile, Megan could rival Lizzie for vivaciousness and beauty combined. Violet had already met Megan a number of times at her bakery, The Rise and Shine.

"Does Caleb have Evie?" Sara asked Megan. On Sara's lap sat a toddler who was about a year old. "Harrison had to go into work today, and that's why this guy is here today hanging with us." Sara kissed the baby's cheek, and he laughed.

"Yeah, he and Evie are going to build a train set today. I told him a ten-month-old isn't going to be much help building anything," said Megan.

"Do you have any children, Violet?" Sara asked.

Violet's smile was sad. "No, but my husband and I talked about it right before he passed away."

"Oh, I'm sorry. I didn't realize—" Sara paled a little.

"It's all right. Really. It's been two years now. I'd rather talk about him in conversation than act like he didn't exist, you know?" Violet tried to smile. She didn't exactly like talking about her husband's death, but sometimes it felt like everyone wanted to forget about him. She and Martha were the only ones keeping his memory alive.

"I'm sorry for your loss," said Abby. Six months pregnant, Abby looked radiant, her hair a glossy brown. Violet had learned that Abby worked as an ER nurse, although she wasn't working as much now that her pregnancy made it harder to stand up all day.

"Thank you." Violet laughed a little. "Good Lord, your faces! You all need some jewelry. Necklaces always make a girl feel better, right?"

When Violet began taking out pieces for everyone to try on, the mood lightened significantly. Violet felt the tension drain from her for the first time in ages. She loved talking about her jewelry and showing women the best pieces for their features and personal styles. Getting paid to do what she loved was the main reason why she'd quit her job to start this business in the first place.

Soon, the women brought their chairs closer to the table where Violet laid the pieces she'd brought that day, including a half dozen necklaces, pairs of earrings, and bracelets. She'd also begun experimenting with making rings, including larger statement pieces with flowers, butterflies, stars, and moons.

"These look like something you could buy at a department store," said Megan as she tried on a pair of silver earrings shaped like leaves. "I'm going to end up buying everything."

"I don't even wear much jewelry, but this makes me want to," said Abby as she tried on a necklace that Violet had constructed out of some silk handkerchiefs she'd found at a flea market in Seattle. "Too bad I can't wear huge necklaces at work."

Rose, with her brown hair tipped with blue, was already trying on three of the bracelets at once. Violet pointed to the one that had delicate floral charms hanging from it. "That one's my favorite," Violet said. "I loved those charms the second I saw them."

"I have way too much jewelry, but I don't think I can say no to these." Rose sighed deeply, causing everyone to laugh.

Bea watched the proceedings avidly, and when she tried to stuff a ring into her mouth, Lizzie snagged it just in time. Bea's face began to screw up, turning red. Violet took one of the necklaces and dangled it in front of Bea, effectively distracting the toddler from her imminent meltdown.

"Look, Bea, isn't it pretty?" Lizzie took the necklace from Violet and put it on Bea.

"Pretty," said Bea. "Want more."

"A girl after my own heart," joked Thea. "We crown you Princess Bea, ruler of us all." She placed another necklace on Bea's head, which the toddler soon pulled off with a frown.

"Don't," said Bea, and everyone laughed.

After they'd finished admiring all of the jewelry, the group chatted and laughed, pairing off into twos and threes. When Thea sat down next to Violet, Violet could feel sweat prickling in the small of her back. She wondered if Thea knew what had happened between her and Ash, and then she dismissed the idea. What younger brother told his *sister* about his sex life?

Thea was tiny, and she seemed to make up for lack of height with her style and her outgoing personality. Tattoos in complicated designs ran up the length of Thea's arms, and a septum piercing in her nose somehow looked charming on her. Violet had never thought that a ring through your nose like a bull was attractive, yet Thea pulled it off. Violet almost envied the woman's confidence to be so daring.

"Do you think you'll open a jewelry store? Like a real location?" asked Thea.

"I've thought about it, but the cost of rent and everything associated with a physical location has just been too much. The cons have outweighed the pros, but I wouldn't say no to it."

"Well, just an FYI: there's an open storefront for rent just a block from my apartment complex." Thea smiled wryly. "It'd be nice to have more than a smoothie shop and a specialty dog store there. A girl can only drink so many smoothies or buy so many dog bones for my nonexistent dog.

"Speaking of dogs..." Thea's smile turned sly, and her expression looked just like Ash's when he'd wanted Violet to go with him to the playground. Violet's heart skipped a beat. "My brother is thinking about getting one, but I told him his place is too small. I thought he should get a cat."

"I've never had a dog," said Violet, nonplussed.

"Neither has Ash. He always wanted one when we were

kids, but, yeah, that wasn't going to happen with our parents in charge. Ash tends to do first, think later, especially when he wants something. I wouldn't be surprised if he ended up getting a huge mutt at the pound and then being surprised that it chews up his furniture."

"Hopefully he'll do some research?" was Violet's pathetic reply. She had no idea where Thea was going with this, and she was too afraid to ask.

"Ash doesn't research. He just *does*. But it tends to get him into hot water. I've seen it happen many times." Thea's eyebrows winged downward. "I just hope that if he gets a dog, he doesn't end up feeling like he made a mistake because the dog is making his life harder. You know what I mean?"

Violet had a distinct feeling that in this scenario, *she* was the dog, and she wasn't sure if she wanted to laugh or cry.

Instead of doing either, Violet said rather sharply, "If the dog makes his life harder, it's his own fault for taking the dog home with him in the first place. Don't blame the dog when the owner didn't think things over beforehand."

Thea blinked before she startled Violet with laughter. "Oh, I'm glad—I like you. You have spunk. None of my brother's other women had any spunk. They were as exciting as lukewarm tapioca."

"Thank you?"

Thea didn't get a chance to respond when Lizzie sat down next to her and started asking Violet all about how she came up with her jewelry designs. When Thea rose, she winked at Violet like she hadn't just basically warned Violet not to hurt her brother.

By the time the party was coming to a close, Violet had sold all but two pieces and had discussed creating customized designs for both Lizzie and Rose. If she could continue to gain more clientele this way, could she actually save her business? Then she wouldn't have to worry Martha or have to confess that she wouldn't be able to help her mother-in-law financially like she'd promised.

The doorbell rang as Violet finished packing everything up. When she heard a masculine voice only yards away, she froze like a deer in headlights.

Oh no. Oh no no no no.

"I just need a folder from Trent," said Ash, who'd been the one to open the door. "Where is he?"

Thea replied, "Upstairs hiding. Come in and say hello to everyone first, though. We're just finishing up."

Violet couldn't let him see her. Getting up, she blurted, "Where's your bathroom?"

"There's one through the kitchen in the back," replied Lizzie, pointing.

Violet grabbed her bag and headed straight toward the kitchen only moments before she heard Ash's voice say, "You guys are having a party and you didn't invite me?"

Violet found the bathroom and locked the door. Hopefully none of the women present would think it was odd that she'd taken her large tote with her into the bathroom. She had to get out of here before Ash saw her.

Then again, more than likely one of the women would

mention she'd been invited here to show her jewelry. Maybe she could hide in the bathroom until Ash left? That seemed the more likely option. She was halfway tempted to sneak out the back door and drive away, but she couldn't be that rude to Lizzie.

Violet could hear the voices from the living room, Ash's lower voice more easily heard than the rest. She heard him say something about *doing work on a Saturday* and then laughter. Violet glanced at the clock on her phone. If she stayed in here too long, someone would come looking for her, and how awkward would that be?

Two minutes passed, then three. When it was getting close to seven minutes and Ash was still talking to people in the living room, Violet muttered under her breath in frustration. *Why is he still here?*

"Hey, Violet, are you in there? I wanted to make sure you were okay," said Abby from through the door.

"I'm fine, just dealing with period stuff," Violet lied, opening the door. Considering Abby was a nurse, Violet didn't feel too weird about saying something like that, even if it was a lie.

"Do you need anything? I probably have pads and tampons in my car." Abby patted her pregnant belly. "Luckily I haven't had to mess with a period for a while now."

"I'm good. Thank you." Violet listened for Ash's voice, and when she heard the front door open and close, she let out a sigh of relief. *Finally.*

Slipping out of the house, she was only steps from her

car door—so close to getting away without running into Ash—when she heard a rustle in the grass. Then: "What a coincidence, running into you."

She bit back a scream of surprise, whirled, and came face-to-face with the man who had haunted her dreams since that night a month ago.

$\mathcal{A}$ sh hadn't seen Violet since she'd sneaked out of his apartment a month ago. He didn't know how she'd managed to avoid him in a town this small—it was almost impressive, in a way.

At the moment, she looked like a cat with its fur standing on end, her eyes blazing. He wondered for the thousandth time what the hell he'd done to freak her out. If the sex hadn't been a big deal to her, why had she gone out of her way to avoid him?

"Hi," she said briskly as she opened her car door. "And goodbye."

He put out a hand to stop her from opening the door. "That's it? What the hell did I do to warrant that kind of a greeting?"

Her shoulders tensed before slumping. "You didn't do

anything," she said, speaking to the car window. "But I need to get home."

Ash wasn't about to let her leave without an explanation. He should've been pleased that she hadn't tried to pursue something more serious. Wasn't that what he always preferred? Violet was the opposite of clingy. She was practically a walking ad for anti-clinginess. If he touched her, he might get repelled from her like the wrong side of a magnet.

"I heard you say inside that you weren't doing anything this evening, and it's only four o'clock, so you don't need to get home to make dinner for your mother-in-law for a few hours," he said. When she turned, her eyebrows raised, he added, "I can also tell when someone is obviously lying."

"What's it to you, then? Yes, I left without saying goodbye that morning. Isn't that your MO? I'm sure you've done that so many times you've lost count."

He gritted his teeth. "I also don't avoid former lovers like they've given me the plague, either."

"Who says I've been avoiding you?" Her gaze slid away as she asked the question.

"It's a small town, sweetheart. The only way to avoid someone is to work very, very hard at it."

Violet blew out an annoyed breath. "Look, that night was great, but it's never going to happen again. That's it. Now, I need to get home—"

"I want to know why it won't happen again." He pressed closer. "And I recommend you tell me now, because

I bet you everything everyone inside is watching us from the living room window right this second."

Violet peered over his shoulder, groaned, and ducked under his arm. She began to walk away without another word.

"Are you just going to leave your car?" Ash jogged to catch up with her. Damn, she was fast. "Where do you live?"

"That's none of your business. Will you stop following me? I don't want to talk to you!"

He slowed down, letting her take the lead. He didn't understand why he needed to know her reasoning. He didn't know why he cared so much that she'd left him that morning without a word. He reached into his pocket to touch the bracelet that she'd left on his pillow and continued to follow her down the street.

"So, you thought that night was great," he began as he caught up with her again. "Is that code for 'terrible' or did you mean that sincerely?"

She rolled her eyes. "I'm not stroking your ego, Ash."

"Too bad. You're so good at stroking."

She stopped in her tracks and glared at him, the color high in her cheeks. "You are the *worst*. I should never have slept with you. It was the worst mistake of my life—"

"I doubt that."

"—and you're obviously just pissed that there's one woman in the whole world who doesn't worship the ground you walk on." She pointed to herself, her voice going low. "Well, surprise! I'm that one woman. Now, leave me alone."

Anger blossomed in his chest. "Stop lying to yourself. I saw the way you looked at me that night. I heard the way you cried out my name when you came not once but twice. And this." He pulled out the bracelet, and her cheeks reddened even more. "You left me a piece of jewelry and a note about how you hoped I had good luck and focus. That doesn't sound like a woman who doesn't care. It sounds like a woman who was terrified of feeling too much and ran at the first opportunity."

She trembled, and the hurt on her face instantly made Ash feel guilty.

You always push too hard. You run right over people's feelings without a second thought. That had been the last text he'd received from his ex-girlfriend Kayla over six months ago. At the time, he'd refused to consider her words, but now he wondered...was there a kernel of truth in them?

"Violet..." He reached up to touch her face, but if she was irritated before, now she was livid.

She slapped his hand away. "Go. To. Hell."

He held up his hands. "I'm sorry. That was out of line." He sighed, pushing his fingers through his hair. "I just—I couldn't stop thinking about you, and it was eating at me, why you left without a word. Because I refuse to believe you didn't feel something that night. I saw your eyes. And this bracelet—" He tightened his fingers around the circle of twine and beads. "You don't make a bracelet for somebody you hate."

"Sure, I do. I do it all the time."

He shook his head, chuckling. "Okay, but never for free."

Crossing her arms, she looked away from him, because she knew he was right.

"Have dinner with me." At her exasperated look, he added, "Lunch. Hell, breakfast. Breakfast is the most platonic meal of the day."

Her lips quirked in the first smile she'd given him. He refused to wonder why that mattered so much to him.

"You are so annoying." She started walking back to her car.

"Is that a yes?"

"No!"

"Is that a no?"

"No!"

That made him laugh. "How about I pick you up tomorrow night for dinner? Does seven work?"

"I thought we were doing breakfast."

"Lunch, then."

She laughed. "Fine, fine! What's your number? I'll text you so you have mine."

Ash wanted to whoop and tell everyone in the damn neighborhood that he'd gotten Violet's phone number. He'd known she hadn't been uninterested, and when she opened her car door, she sent him a sultry look under her lashes that set his whole body ablaze.

~

"IF IT'S NOT A DATE, then what is it?" Martha asked as Violet got ready for her lunch-date-that-wasn't-a-date the following day. "Because I'm pretty sure going out with a man is a date. Wait, is he gay? Is that it?"

Violet laughed. "No, he's not gay. It just isn't a date. We're friends."

"Well, you sure are wearing a nice outfit for a friend." Martha tittered as she left Violet to finish primping.

It's not a date if I say it isn't, Violet kept telling herself even as anticipation simmered in her blood. Running into Ash yesterday had been a disaster, yet when she'd realized that he'd been totally sincere and, God almighty, that he'd been hurt at her running out on him... she couldn't have been more amazed if someone had told her aliens had landed on her front lawn.

But today was just lunch. Sedate, normal, platonic lunch. Nobody could get hot and bothered over a turkey sandwich. Then again, this was Ash Younger. He could probably get a woman hot and bothered with a bologna sandwich if he so much as sent her a heated look.

"I'm heading out. Have fun! Don't do anything I wouldn't!" called Martha as she left for her own lunch date with Dennis. Not only was it going to be a lunch date, but Martha and Dennis were going to some bingo game that would last all afternoon and apparently had some huge prizes if you won.

Twenty minutes later, there was a knock on the front door. Expecting Ash, Violet opened the door with a huge smile that soon deflated when she saw that it wasn't Ash. It was a total stranger. And he didn't look particularly nice, either.

"Is there a Violet Fielding in residence?"

"That's me. Is something wrong?"

He handed her a document that read SUMMONS at the top in huge black letters. "I don't understand," she said weakly.

"You've been summoned. Everything you'll need to know is in the document. Have a nice afternoon."

Violet could only nod, totally flabbergasted. She knew she'd gotten behind on her payments for her business loan, but a lawsuit? Terror shot through her as she read the summons. The legal jargon made her head hurt until she just wanted to slump onto the floor, roll up into a ball, and cry her eyes out.

But apparently today could only go from bad to worse. As she was about to close her door, she heard footsteps and watched in horror as Ash walked up to the house. Based on his expression, he'd seen—and probably had heard—everything.

Violet wanted to melt into the floor. She wanted to slam the door, lock it, and never ever come out again. She didn't need Ash pitying her, or worse, judging her.

The summons document was crumpled in Violet's hand when Ash approached her, his forehead creased.

"Did you hear all of that?" she asked hoarsely.

He nodded, grimacing. "I didn't mean to eavesdrop— I'd just gotten out of my car and I saw you had someone at your door—"

"It's fine. What does it matter that you got to watch one of the most humiliating moments of my life?" She laughed, but it was a bitter sound. "I'm an asshole, but I don't think I'd be good company for lunch today. Can I get a rain check?"

"What? Yes, of course." To Violet's dismay, Ash didn't turn around and leave: he followed her inside the house and into the living room. "I'm assuming you were served with a lawsuit?"

She handed him the notice. "Might as well know everything. I can't be any more embarrassed than I am already."

Ash took it gingerly and as he scanned the words, his forehead creased even more, his eyes narrowed. "How much are you in debt, Violet?"

"I don't know." She collapsed onto the couch and rubbed her temples. "Last time I checked it was close to thirty thousand, but I haven't looked in a while."

"How long is 'a while'?"

She grimaced. "Six months?"

"Jesus." He sat down on the couch next to her and set the summons on the coffee table. "You can't ignore debt. It doesn't just disappear."

"I'm well aware. I'm not saying it was a *good* decision." Under her breath, she muttered, "I seem to make a lot of bad decisions lately."

Ash didn't take the bait, though. "How long has this been going on? Do you have enough funds for a lawyer?"

She had a feeling setting herself on fire would be preferable to this conversation.

I told you this wasn't a good idea. William's words echoed inside her mid, making her stomach knot. He'd never loved the idea of her starting her own business because he had known very well her money management skills were lacking. When they'd married, she'd had credit card debt that had grown large enough that it had made it difficult for them to buy a house until they'd paid it off. William had been afraid she'd destroy the credit they'd worked so hard to build if she started a business. He'd only agreed to sign off on a business loan if she let him manage the books.

After William had died, the books had fallen to her. And look what had happened: she was being sued by a collection agency for not paying her loan back.

"If I had money for a lawyer, I'd have money to pay off my debt, wouldn't I?" Realizing she sounded like a jerk, she sighed. "I'm sorry. This isn't your problem and you don't need to hear me bitching and moaning." She sent him a tremulous smile. "I'll figure it out. I always do."

Ash was silent for so long that a prickle of unease ran up Violet's spine.

"Who's doing your books?" he finally asked.

"I am, and badly. Numbers have never been my strength. I can sell jewelry and make money, but then somehow the money seems to just...disappear." She frowned and then groaned. "I don't even have a retail location! You wouldn't think this would be so hard."

"True, but you have inventory, shipping costs, production costs. You run a website too, right?" He stroked his chin. "I can look at your books, if you'd like. I can at least figure out a way for you to budget so you can pay off this loan."

Her heart flip-flopped. "Ash, that's very sweet, but I can't afford to pay for an accountant right now. I can barely keep my head above water as it is. And you have your own job managing your brother's books—I can't ask you to take time away from that."

"I'd do it for free. I wouldn't charge you a dime, especially if I can't guarantee I can really make any difference." His voice was gentle—so gentle that Violet almost couldn't believe this was the same man who'd refused to take no for an answer yesterday afternoon. The same man who'd accused her of being too scared to look what they had in the face.

"I can't ask you to do that. It's too much," she protested.

"You aren't asking me: I'm offering." He smiled wryly. "And what is there to lose?"

"It's not that. It's that you'll be working for free when I doubt you have the time to spare."

"Trent will survive. I just won't tell him."

Violet rubbed her damp palms against her jeans. God, if Ash could help her, if she could get out from under this without drowning? The thought was unimaginable, and yet, now it seemed almost within reach with him offering to help. A lump formed in her throat.

She took a shaky breath. "Okay, then yes. I'd love for you to look over my books, although I warn you, the last two years of them are a mess."

His smile was radiant, and it sent a frisson of heat through Violet's body. That smile of his could make her do anything he wanted. She hated that she was so weak for him still.

Ash said, "Great. Stop by my office at the Fainting Goat this week with everything. I'm usually in during the afternoons. We'll figure this out. In the meantime, you should call the collection agency and try to get terms for repayment. Tell them you can pay a small amount every month. If they can get any money from you, they will. They prefer that to messing with a lawsuit and getting no money."

Hope was a dangerous emotion right now, but she let herself enjoy it—for now. "Thank you, I will. If it's okay, I'll work on that this afternoon instead of going to lunch."

"Then that just means you owe me dinner later," he said, touching her shoulder with an encouraging smile.

8

*A*sh swore when he couldn't find the green folder with the documents he needed. He shuffled through the twenty other folders on his desk and the seemingly endless piles of papers, getting to the point where he was tempted to dump everything onto the floor and set it on fire.

It was twelve fifty in the afternoon, and Violet had texted him two hours prior to say she would be stopping by with her books by one o'clock. He'd glanced at his watch at least half a dozen times since then. *12:51.* Nine minutes to find this folder for Trent so he wouldn't be lurking when Violet arrived. The last thing Ash needed was his older brother sticking his giant nose into his business, which was one of Trent's favorite things to do.

"Hey, do you have that folder yet? Whoa, what the hell

happened in here?" Trent surveyed the mess on Ash's desk. "Don't you have bins and shit to organize this stuff? How much am I paying you anyway?"

"You're paying me nothing, as you know, and when you have twenty thousand pieces of paper and folders, two bins isn't going to make a damn bit of difference." When Ash moved a cup of cold coffee off a piece of paper, he found the green folder he'd been searching for. "Here it is," he said as he handed the folder to Trent. "Take it."

"A little tense today? Was something up with our tax return?"

"No, that's fine. It's got nothing to do with the books here, actually. Everything was in order and I sent it all to the IRS without a hitch."

When Ash heard footsteps in the hallway, he tensed, waiting for Violet to come around the corner. But it was just one of the sous chefs going to the restroom.

Ash hadn't planned on offering to look over Violet's books when he'd overheard her receiving that summons. He wasn't hardhearted, but he wasn't particularly into charity, either. Yet when he'd seen the humiliation and despair in her eyes, he'd wanted to do anything in his power to eradicate them from her gaze. He'd offered to look at her books before he'd even considered why Violet's happiness mattered so much to him.

"Wait, if this isn't about work, then what is it about?" Trent folded his arms across his chest. Ever since he'd gotten married and had a kid, Trent's fatherly shtick with his younger siblings had only worsened. Ash wished his older brother would stop meddling in his life for once.

"None of your damn business." Ash stuffed some folders into a drawer so his desk didn't look so messy. It only slightly worked.

"You're growly, grumpy, and you have circles under your eyes." Trent's eyes narrowed. "It's a woman, isn't it?"

When Ash refused to answer, Trent laughed. "Oh, how the tables have turned! You were on my ass for getting back together with Lizzie, and now here you are, practically ripping your hair out over a woman. This is amazing."

Ash glared up at Trent. "Are you done yet?"

"Hell no. I'm just getting started. Who is it?" When Ash flipped him off, Trent just shrugged. "I'll get it out of you eventually. Better yet, I'll ask Thea, who probably knows the woman's Social Security number at this point. Can I give you some advice?"

"No," was Ash's deadpan reply.

"If you really like her, don't fuck it up. Think before you act."

"Wow, great advice! Oh wait, except I'm not the one who accidentally got a woman pregnant *twice*."

"Oh, I'm sorry. I didn't mean to interrupt." Violet stepped just inside the door, holding her purse close to her side.

Ash had to bite back laughter at the blush creeping onto Trent's cheeks. Ash knew his older brother would get revenge for Ash's remark, but Ash didn't care about anything Trent could do to him. His entire focus was on Violet.

"No, you're not interrupting," said Ash smoothly. "My brother was just leaving."

"I'm Trent Younger." Trent held out his hand, shaking Violet's with a slight divot in his forehead now. "Have I met you before?"

"Yes, at your house. Your wife hosted my jewelry party."

"Oh, of course. I'm terrible with names and faces." He grinned self-deprecatingly.

"There were a lot of people there." Violet smiled as she added, "You have a lovely restaurant."

"I don't know if I'd call throwing out drunks at three a.m. lovely, but thank you." Trent sent Ash a look that said *this isn't over* before departing.

Ash shut the door and motioned for Violet to sit. "I should've asked—do you want anything to drink? Water, coffee?"

"No, I'm fine." She still clutched her bag, and her gaze darted around his office. If the tension in her shoulders indicated anything, she was definitely not excited to be here. "I just realized that I can't accept your offer. I mean, it's almost tax day. You have to be completely slammed with work here."

He smiled gently at her. "No, I've already filed everything. I prefer to get everything in before the deadline."

"Oh." She deflated. "Well, if you're sure—"

"I'm sure, but are you? Did something else happen?"

Violet shook her head. "No, nothing. At least, nothing bad." She blew out a frustrated breath. "I'm sorry. I sound like such an ungrateful ninny. I really appreciate you offering to help. Even if you do have time, it's still work." Opening her purse, she began pulling out folders, papers, receipts, and a few USB drives, placing them on Ash's desk. "That's everything."

He flipped through some of the documents, many of which were handwritten. Jesus, was this a receipt tallied on a napkin? Nothing was in order, and many of the documents had no dates on them. He sighed inwardly, but seeing this mess only proved that he'd done the right thing in offering to help Violet.

"My husband, he did the books before he passed away. I think everything should be scanned and uploaded onto the USB drives, but I haven't checked. That doesn't include the last two years, though. I'm afraid all of this is my mess. It just got out of hand, and when things get overwhelming I tend to ignore them."

"I understand. I'll start putting things in order, although I'll probably need your help with deciphering some of these notes." He peered more closely at another handwritten note. "Is this your husband's handwriting? It looks too messy for a woman's."

She peered at the note then laughed. "No, that's my handwriting. Did I mention my handwriting is basically chicken scratch?"

Ash's head was starting to hurt, looking at this huge

mess on his desk, but Violet's hopeful expression was all he needed to convince himself how important this all was.

"I'll get started on this this afternoon. Like I said before, I can't guarantee that I can figure out what's going on or offer any advice, but at least you'll be organized going forward."

"That's enough for me. You've taken a huge weight off my shoulders. I really appreciate it. Thank you."

It wasn't very often someone expressed gratitude so sincerely for something he'd done for them. *You're getting in deep here*, his mind said. *Do you know what you're doing?*

No, but fuck me if I care.

Yes, he was helping out someone who needed it. If that person just so happened to be the woman he'd slept with a month ago and then couldn't stop thinking about when she'd basically disappeared, well, he'd deal with it.

"You're welcome. Were you able to get a payment plan in place?" he asked.

"Yes, and thank you for the suggestion. They said as long as I paid a set amount each month, they wouldn't pursue the lawsuit further. I just have to scrimp and save, which I was already doing." She blew out a breath. "It wasn't like this when my husband was alive, I promise."

Ash was sorting through the mound of documents she'd handed him, although at the mention of her husband, his ears perked up. What kind of a man had Violet fallen for and married? He was suddenly beyond curious—but just curious. There was no other reason why he'd want to know about her husband.

"How long were you married?" He asked the question casually as he began sorting. "It can't have been that long, considering how young you are."

"Such a flatterer. We were married for eight years. We met in college, got engaged after graduation, and then were married." Her smile was sad. "He was the love of my life."

Ash barely restrained a flinch at that declaration. *Christ, why does it matter? Of course she loved her husband, you idiot.*

"I'm sorry for your loss." The words were difficult for him to get out.

"Thank you." Her gaze turned far away. "He was the practical one. He didn't want me to start this business because he knew how bad I was at numbers. He only agreed to cosign for the business loan if I agreed to let him do the books."

For some reason, that bit of information made Ash frown inwardly. He understood wanting your spouse to do things correctly, but telling your wife you wouldn't let her do something that meant so much to her?

Not your marriage, not your monkeys, not your zoo. Don't say a damn thing, man.

"I guess he came around?" was Ash's neutral reply.

"He did. I can be very persuasive when I need to be. Everything was going great until the last few months before William's death." She hesitated. "We were having some issues again, right before the accident. Mostly because the business was going south and the numbers weren't adding up. William thought I should close up shop, so to speak. I didn't want to. Our last conversation was an argument. If I regret anything, I regret that the most."

Her voice sounded choked now, and Ash looked up to see her brushing tears away. Her smile was sad now. "Don't let anyone you love leave when you're angry with them. You never know—it might be the last time you see them."

"I'll remember that."

They gazed at each other, the moment taut, and Ash wanted to take her in his arms and tell her she didn't need to worry anymore. He didn't know why he wanted—no, needed—to take care of her when he'd never thought he had a care-taking bone in his body. He'd lived his life mostly independently, flitting from woman to woman. He had his family, of course, and he had male friends, but nothing like what his brother Trent had with Lizzie.

And in that moment, he craved something more to such an extent that he slammed the feeling down, down, down, into the recesses of his brain until he could believe it had disappeared.

"Well, I should get going." Violet rose from her chair and held out her hand. "Thank you, again. Let me know if there's any way I can help."

He went around the desk and took her hand, squeezing her fingers. "Of course. I'll text you about that dinner date."

"Really? You're still going on about that?"

He grinned. "Hey, you cancelled lunch, so that means dinner now. You can't get out of this one so easily. Unless there's someone else who might be suing you?"

"Ha-ha, you're hilarious." But her eyes sparkled as she waved goodbye and left his office, her ass looking particularly amazing in the tight jeans she was wearing.

Damn her for being so gorgeous, he thought with a groan before he got back to work.

9

*V*iolet waved as her sister Vera's face popped up on her phone for their monthly video chat. Someone yelled and then there was a crash, but Vera just shrugged.

"Ethan has a new soccer ball and I told him"—she looked over her shoulder—"not to play with it *inside*. Ethan Lucas, if you break another vase I'm going to put you up for adoption!"

"Yeah right!" Ethan called from the background.

Vera rolled her eyes. Two years older than Violet, Vera didn't look like her sister at all. She was shorter, with dark brown hair and eyes, although she and Violet had a similar smile. Vera had married a decade ago and had two children, Isabella and Ethan, who were eight and six, respectively. Violet hadn't really understood her sister's attraction to the staid and quiet Jim, but as far as Violet knew, their marriage had been relatively happy.

"So, what's new with you?" asked Vera. "How's the business going?"

Violet had told her sister about the business's financial issues, although now she didn't know how to tell her that Ash Younger was looking at her books without telling her sister about Ash in the first place. She'd neglected to tell Vera that she'd had a one-night stand with a younger man a month ago. Vera wasn't a prude, but even she would be shocked that Violet had done something so out of character.

"I actually found someone who would look over my books at no cost," hedged Violet.

"Is he an actual accountant?"

"Yes, he is. What, did you think I'd hire some random off the street?"

"I wouldn't put it past you." Vera frowned. "How'd you find someone that nice? No one's that nice."

"He's a friend of a friend. Actually, he's the brother-in-law of the woman I told you about—Lizzie Younger? I just had my jewelry party at her house."

"Huh. Well, he must be a saint, considering what a mess your books are. I have to ask, how old is this very saintly guy?"

"Old enough."

"Is he handsome?"

"Vera!"

Vera's smile was sly. "So he is handsome. That explains it all. Is he single, too?"

Violet sniffed. "I'm not having this conversation."

"Then you're going to have to hang up to get out of it. Based on how red you're turning, he's handsome *and* single. Did you pay him a late-night visit to get this favor from him?" she joked.

When Violet blushed bright red and spluttered, though, Vera gasped. "No! Violet! Did you sleep with him and you didn't tell me? You're in so much trouble!"

Knowing that Vera was like a bloodhound that'd caught the scent of prey, Violet told her about Ash, including the night they'd met and how she'd gone home with him.

Vera's eyes sparkled. "How was the sex? Good?"

"I'm not giving you details!"

"Oh, come on. The most exciting thing going on right now is Jim's root canal for Thursday. I need some smutty details."

"It was..." *Amazing, mind-blowing, unforgettable?* "It was really good."

"That means it was terrible. No wonder you didn't want to talk about it."

Violet laughed. "No, I mean, it was better than good. Great. Amazing. He's a guy who knows what he's doing, I'll say that."

Frowning, Vera put her chin on her hand. "Okay, then are you seeing each other? If the sex is amazing and he's kind enough to do your books for free, then he must be a good guy. Hell, if you don't want him, I'll take him."

"I heard that," said a male voice behind Vera, which Violet recognized as Vera's husband Jim's voice.

"Vera, is Jim listening to this conversation?"

Jim, his glasses perched on his nose, peered into Vera's phone and waved at Violet. "Hi, Violet. I'm just going upstairs."

Violet groaned in humiliation while Vera laughed. "He won't say anything," said Vera. "You know him. Now, why aren't you dating this guy? I'm confused."

How did Violet explain that Ash was a total playboy who didn't do relationships? *Except he told me he couldn't stop thinking about me. What kind of a playboy continues to pursue a woman he's already slept with?* It made no sense.

Maybe he was just being nice to get her into bed again. It seemed like an awful lot of effort, but Violet hadn't always understood men. Her only real experience with men had been with William, and in comparison to Ash, the two men were like night and day.

"Ash just isn't the guy for me," Violet said, trying to explain something she couldn't explain to herself. "He's younger than me."

"How much younger?"

"Five years."

"That's not that much. Okay, so he's a little younger than you...? That's it?"

Violet blew out a breath. "No, he's a one-and-done kind of guy. He has a reputation around here for it."

"So much that he offered to look at your books for free? Come on, Violet. He's totally into you."

Those words should've excited Violet, but oddly enough, they only scared her. It had only been two years since William had died. How could she even consider moving on already? It was too fast, too soon.

"Nothing's going to happen. That's all there is to say," Violet said firmly.

"Oh honey." Vera's voice gentled. "I know how much you miss William. We all do. But you can't not live your own life, either. He would've wanted you to be happy. How long are you going to lock yourself away from the world? From dating? From maybe even remarrying?"

"I can't think about that. It's too soon."

"Vi, it's been two years. Not two months. Years."

"And how long would it take you to get over Jim?" she snapped.

"I'm not saying get over William. You don't get over your husband's death, but you can rebuild your life. You'll always have a place for William in your heart, but your heart is big enough for another love, too. I know it is. Don't push this Ash guy away out of fear, because I think you'll regret it."

After she and Vera had hung up, Violet sat on her bed, her heart heavy. Was her sister right? Martha had certainly said the same thing, that Violet couldn't stop living life because William was gone. Tears choked Violet's throat. *How can I move on without you, William?*

Their wedding photos sat on her dresser, and she brushed a thumb over the glass covering them. In one photo, they were both laughing. Violet couldn't remember what had made them laugh like that. William had looked especially handsome in his tuxedo. Although he hadn't been as handsome or as tall as Ash, he'd been handsome in his own way. He'd had kind eyes, and he'd told the cheesiest jokes. He'd told Violet one on their first date and she'd fallen for him right then and there.

William had worked as an electrical engineer, although when his company had begun laying employees off when the economy had started to collapse, William had been transferred from position to position, taking multiple pay cuts in the process. Violet's idea of starting her business perhaps hadn't been the greatest, considering the timing, but she'd been making pennies as an administrative assistant at a marketing firm. She'd hated how stifling that job had been. Entrepreneurship, with all of its potential pitfalls, had seemed infinitely preferable to being stuck in a cubicle for the rest of her life.

Violet touched William's smiling face in the photo. The first few years of their marriage, before all the financial and job issues, had been the best years of her life. Things had started to sour, though, although Violet knew that a lot of it had been her fault. If she hadn't been so insistent on starting her business, if she'd learned how to manage her money better, if she hadn't pushed and pushed...

She wiped a tear from her cheek. Regrets wouldn't do any good now, would they? William was gone. She couldn't tell him how sorry she was. That last argument had been the most volatile.

"You always do what you want. You never think about

me. You're so focused on this business that it's like I don't exist." William's words had pierced her like an arrow to the heart, and, angry and hurt, she'd lashed back.

"You've never supported me or the business," she threw back.

He scoffed. "Are you serious? When I do your books every year? How is that not supporting you?"

"You do the books for *yourself*. Not for me. Because you're so convinced I couldn't do it, or couldn't find someone better to do it."

William's cheeks reddened. "That's unfair, and you know it." Scowling, he grabbed his coat and put his shoes on. "You know what, I'm not listening to this. I'm going out."

"In the pouring-down rain?"

When he didn't respond, Violet's vision turned red, anger spiking inside her. "You know what, run. That's what you're good at. And while you're at it, don't come back! I don't need to keep trying to convince you that I'm not some moron when I'm more than capable of running a successful business!"

William's eyes blazed. "If you don't want me to come back, I won't." He slammed the front door behind him, and a moment later, the sound of screeching tires filled the night.

That was the last time she saw William alive.

When her phone rang hours later, she didn't pick it up because she assumed it was William wanting to tell her how wrong she was. Her phone went to voicemail, then promptly started ringing again. Annoyed, she frowned when she saw that the caller ID wasn't William. The voice on the other end wasn't one she recognized—but it was a voice that would haunt her dreams for the rest of her life.

Your husband has been in an accident. I'm so sorry, but he didn't make it.

He'd been T-boned by another driver at an intersection. It had been raining hard, and the streets had been slick. The driver who'd hit him had run the red light and had slammed into the driver's side of William's car. The driver had survived with only a broken arm, while William had died on impact.

Tears fell down Violet's cheeks in rivers now as she gazed at her wedding photos. She wiped them away, but they kept coming. The photos in her hand blurred behind her veil of tears.

How can I move on when you're not here anymore? she thought. It was easy enough for Vera to say those words. Did her sister have any idea how much Violet would like to move on but couldn't?

"Violet? Are you home?" Martha called as she closed the front door.

Violet hastily wiped her tears away and set the photos on her dresser, but when Martha came into her bedroom, she saw Violet's red eyes and wet face and knew without asking what she'd been doing.

"Oh, honey, what is it?"

Violet started crying again as she sat down on the bed with Martha holding her. Martha was half Violet's size, but

Violet still felt safe in her arms. She let herself cry a little longer as Martha touched her hair, soothing her but never trying to stop her from crying.

Violet eventually sat up, and Martha handed her a tissue from her purse. "Now, what was that all about?" Martha asked.

"I'm just sad today. I miss him."

Martha's own eyes glittered with tears. "I do too. I had a dream about him last night. We were all eating dinner here and you made some weird dish with Brussels sprouts. William hated Brussels sprouts, you know."

"I remember. No matter how I made them, he couldn't even swallow one without spitting it out."

Martha rubbed Violet's back, and Violet sighed, suddenly exhausted. "Vera thinks I've put my life on hold," she admitted. "She thinks I should start dating again."

"And I agree with her." When Violet tensed, Martha added, "You don't have to *date*-date. You can just...go out. You can't lock yourself away, Violet. It won't bring him back."

"I know, but it feels like..." She shook her head. "It feels like a betrayal, like I've forgotten him."

"Of course not. You'll never forget him, and I'll never forget him, either. I think about him always, but every day it gets a little easier. The grief never goes away. But every day that passes is a little easier."

"I'm so afraid I'm forgetting things about him. I couldn't remember his favorite color earlier today." Violet sniffled. "I don't think I'm ready to date."

"Maybe not. That's okay, too. But don't hold yourself back out of fear or guilt. It's one thing not to be ready; it's another to avoid something because it scares you."

Violet hugged Martha, inhaling her perfume. "I'm glad I moved here to be with you."

"The day you told me you'd be coming here, it was like I finally saw a light at the end of the tunnel for the first time since William's death."

The two women fell silent, remembering the person they'd both loved so much.

"Where were you today?" asked Violet suddenly. "I didn't think you had an appointment."

"I told you that my doctor's appointment was moved, didn't I? Well, it doesn't matter. He says my blood sugar was a bit too high but that it can be managed."

Guilt twisted Violet's gut. She'd been so wrapped up in her own little world that she'd forgotten the person she'd come to Fair Haven to help.

"'A bit too high'? Do you remember the number?"

Martha shrugged. "No, I can't."

Violet had a feeling her mother-in-law wasn't being completely truthful, and that only made Violet resolve to go to as many doctor's appointments with Martha as she could. Martha was too neglectful of her own health. Violet had to be the one to make sure Martha controlled her diabetes. Because if she lost Martha, Violet knew she wouldn't survive it.

She'd already lost William. Another blow like that would cripple her.

*a*sh rolled his neck and checked the time. He'd been working on Violet's books for over three hours now, and his eyes were blurry from staring at incomprehensible spreadsheets on his computer and mounds of indecipherable notes and receipts. Her husband might have taken care of the books, but he'd done a shit job of it.

Going back to the beginning, Ash had yet to figure out how William had come up with his numbers. There were acronyms throughout that were never explained, and Ash could also find no records of many expenses. All of it had given him a raging headache.

Shutting his laptop, he rubbed his eyes. He wished he could give Violet good news, and he felt stupid for thinking he'd be able to figure things out quickly. *Pride comes before the fall.* He'd told Violet he couldn't guarantee anything. But that didn't mean he hadn't thought he wouldn't untangle this mess, either.

Ash wished he could wring William's neck. It wasn't just jealousy that made him feel that way: from William's lack of support for Violet to his shit job of managing Violet's books, Ash had come to the conclusion that William hadn't deserved Violet one bit. Of course, Ash didn't know the ins and outs of their marriage. He was basing his assumption on snippets of information, but that didn't stop him from imagining the scenario of wringing William's neck regardless.

Someone knocked on his apartment door before entering. "It's me," said Thea. She came in carrying two pizza boxes. When she saw that his coffee table was covered with papers, she raised an eyebrow. "You were sure having fun today."

He laughed. Pushing the papers into some semblance of a neat pile, he got up to get plates and drinks for them both. Thea hadn't texted to say she'd be coming over, but Thea rarely did. She came up with an idea and a minute later, she did it.

"I got vegan pizza for me, disgusting normal pizza for you," she said.

"So, you got me the edible pizza?" Ash piled three pieces of the meat lover's supreme pizza onto his plate. How did the sweet scent of cheese and grease always make a person feel better? Pizza could cure the world's evils with just one bite.

"Eating animals is inhumane, but I already knew that

you were evil." Since becoming vegan, Thea had embraced the lifestyle with a verve that only served to amuse Ash. He made a point to tease her about it as much as she made a point to chastise him for eating meat.

"How many protests did you attend this week? Did you throw red paint on anyone?" he asked.

She wrinkled her nose. "I only went to one, and it was just me and two other people."

"What was the protest?"

"A chicken farm outside the city with horrible conditions." Thea's face fell. "You should've seen all those chickens, stuffed in that barn and so fat with growth hormones that they can't walk—"

Ash held up a hand. "Not while I'm eating."

"You mean not while you're eating those very chickens?"

He took a huge bite of pizza. "Exactly."

Ash had a feeling that Thea had embraced veganism and everything that came along with it because her life was in stasis at the moment. She hated her job as a receptionist, and although she was a talented artist, she hadn't yet been able to make a living from her art. It didn't help that she was so protective of her art—which consisted mostly of graphic novels—that she wouldn't even let her family read or look at her work.

Thea was a total bleeding heart: she tended to try to save anyone and anything she could. Ash couldn't judge her for it, although he'd never tell her as much. A younger brother had to keep those kinds of opinions to himself.

After they finished eating, Thea pointed to the pile of papers. "Doing work on the weekends again? I thought you had already finished everything with the restaurants' taxes."

"I did. This isn't related to that."

When he didn't explain, Thea frowned. "Are you doing someone's taxes for them?" Her eyes gleamed, and before Ash could react, she'd snagged a number of the papers and began rifling through them. "White Dahlia Jewelry—*oh*. I get it now. So you're doing Violet Fielding's taxes now? I hope you're charging her a pretty penny."

He gritted his teeth. "It's none of your damn business." He took the papers from her and returned them to the pile.

"Don't tell me that the infamous Ash Younger, playboy extraordinaire, the man who wouldn't drive me to the mall as a teenager without me agreeing to buy you something in return, is doing something for free." She started laughing. "No way. You're doing Violet's books for *free*? Wow. The sex must've been really amazing for you to agree to that."

"Thea," he growled in warning.

"Hey, I'm just saying. Nothing wrong with being nice and charitable for once. I'm happy to see that you have a flesh-and-blood heart. I thought for sure it was made of stone."

"I'm just helping her out. She needed it, and I offered. That's it. I'm not a complete asshole."

"Debatable. And considering what a huge mess this is, just from looking at it, I have a feeling this is a massive favor you're doing for her. You must really like this woman."

Ash wanted to push his sister out the nearest window.

Or duct-tape her mouth shut. Why did older sisters have to be so damn nosy? He didn't exactly pry into the details of her love life. Then again, Thea hadn't dated much in the last few years, and the guys she had dated had been such wimps that Ash hadn't had to threaten to beat them up if they hurt Thea, since she'd been the one to end things every single time.

"She's nice," he hedged, finishing off his beer. "Want another beer?"

"No, I'm good. She *is* nice. I was at her jewelry party Saturday. It's funny—when I mentioned you, she suddenly stopped being so chatty." Thea's smile widened. "She seemed like she'd rather talk about cockroaches than talk about you."

Ash was going to kill his sister, and no one could blame him for it. "Thea, just drop it."

"No, no, I'm just saying that I know there's *something* between you two, and the fact that you're here, stewing about a woman when you never ever stew, is probably the greatest thing since the invention of the toaster oven." She laughed and fell back against the couch. "Mostly because seeing you squirm is way too satisfying."

Ash got up to get another beer for himself. Staring into the depths of his fridge, he once again wondered why the hell he was doing this for Violet. Why being around her mattered so much. Why he couldn't stop thinking about her. Why he dreamed of their one night together and yearned for many, many more nights with her.

He slammed the refrigerator door closed, the sound of it rattling immensely satisfying.

"If we're going to talk about my love life," he said as he sat back down, "we might as well talk about yours. Fair is fair."

Thea shrugged. "Nothing to talk about."

"Exactly. How long has it been? Three years?"

"Four," she mumbled. "I've been busy."

He snorted. "With answering phones? Come on, admit it: you're just as fucked up as I am with shit like this. Our parents did a number on us all. We're damaged goods. So what?"

Thea's expression turned somber. "Is that what you think? That we're too damaged to have something real?"

Ash fell silent. He'd always thought so. He'd told himself that love wasn't in the cards for him, and he'd been fine with that. Love was complicated and messy and dramatic. He'd seen how Trent had been torn apart when Lizzie had run off, how he'd yearned for her for years. Was all that pain worth it in the end? Ash didn't know. It sounded like a lot of bullshit to him.

"You saw how Mom turned out when Dad didn't love her like she loved him." He shrugged. "It ended badly."

"That's one way to put it. But do you really think that was love between them? I think it was a lot of manipulation and abuse. You don't hurt people you claim to love."

Ash wanted to slap himself. Why had he brought up their parents? He thought of his mother, of her battered face after his father had hit her, how she'd cry in her room for hours, and how nothing he or any of his siblings did could make her stop crying. How she'd been alive one morning and dead from an intentional overdose by the afternoon.

How their father had gotten meaner and meaner until none of them except Trent had gone near him. The first time all of the siblings had been in the same room with their father was when he'd been dying. That had been two years ago now.

His ex-girlfriend Kayla's text rang in his mind again. Kayla had been gorgeous, but she'd been at loose ends for years and had gotten clingier and clingier with him. Ash had believed that she'd wanted to be in a relationship with him because he seemed like a good source of security for her. In an effort to help Kayla, he'd gotten her a job at a local restaurant and had found an apartment for her without consulting her. Kayla had thrown both offers in his face and had broken up with him right then.

You always push too hard, she'd texted later. He did things without thinking of the consequences; he thought he could order people's lives because he was arrogant enough to think he knew better than them. Everything Kayla had said had pricked at him until he felt like he was covered in cuts and nicks.

Had he pushed too hard, or had Kayla simply overreacted? Now he didn't even know. Lately, he didn't know if he could trust his own judgment.

"Why does everyone think that having something real is

that important?" he asked. "I don't need marriage and kids to make me happy. Not everyone is like Trent."

"True, but it's one thing if you don't want that. It's another if you deny yourself it because you're convinced you don't deserve it."

Those words rang in his mind after Thea left, and he began to look through Violet's books again. Although he was exhausted, there was something about these books that nagged him.

As he looked further into the entries, he realized that not all of them had been done by William. There were at least three other bookkeepers who'd assisted on some level, some doing a better job than others. Ash frowned. Had William hired help without Violet knowing? And more importantly, had one of these bookkeepers cheated Violet out of her own hard-earned money?

Ash began taking notes, trying to follow the clues. He hoped he was wrong, but as evening turned into night and he turned red-eyed with fatigue, he became more convinced that someone had skimmed money from Violet's business.

11

*V*iolet scanned the occupants at the bakery, The Rise and Shine, and let out a breath of relief that Ash hadn't arrived yet. It wasn't that she didn't want to see him, but at the same time, she needed to prepare herself anytime she was around him.

Everything he did reminded her of their night together. He could do something as benign as tap his finger against his knee, and suddenly she'd be transported back to when he'd parted *her* knees and had sunk between them...

"What can I get you?" a girl with dark brown glasses and pink hair asked Violet. The girl smiled, showing perfectly straight white teeth.

"An Americano with room for cream, please."

"Cream in an Americano? I'm going to have to write you up," Ash said over her shoulder.

Violet jumped a little and whirled to face him. "You scared me!"

"You didn't hear the front doorbell jingle?" He grinned.

She'd been so lost in her thoughts that she hadn't heard anything. Blushing, she turned back to the cashier and paid for her coffee, avoiding Ash's amused eyes. He ordered and came over to the table Violet had snagged in the back of the shop. A number of people were already there, but luckily, she didn't recognize anyone she knew. The last thing she needed was anyone gossiping about her being with Ash.

"Your text last night kind of freaked me out," said Violet, trying to sound lighthearted and failing. "I hope my books weren't that bad."

Ash's grin quickly fell away, his forehead creasing. Taking out his laptop from his bag, he moved his chair closer to Violet's so he could show her some spreadsheets. She inhaled his scent, the hair on the back of her neck prickling. Her heart thumped so loudly that she almost didn't hear what he was telling her.

"The numbers, they just wouldn't add up," he was saying, pointing to one of the spreadsheet's cells. "It took a while because everything was such a huge mess, but I hate to tell you this..." He took a deep breath. "Someone was skimming from your business. Money is missing."

It was silly, really, but she hadn't expected to hear that. She'd expected to hear Ash scold her for her poor bookkeeping, or for him to recommend how to do things better. She'd thought that it was all just a mess, not that someone had been *stealing* from her. She felt the ground shift under her until it took her a moment to regain her bearings. North was south, east was west, and nothing made any sense.

"Do you know who it was?" Her mouth was dry as she asked. She felt a bit like she wanted to throw up.

"Did you know your husband hired bookkeepers to help? Because I found evidence of at least three handling the accounts."

"Yes, I knew. I mean, it was for such a short time with each one that honestly I'd forgotten he'd even hired any, but it must have been one of them. How much money do you think they stole?"

"I'm not sure, but I'm guessing at least ten thousand." At Violet's groan, he put a hand on her shoulder. "If these bookkeepers were around for such a short time, are you sure…?" His voice trailed away.

She stared at him. When he looked away, she realized what he'd been asking. "Are you asking me if *William* had something to do with this?" The thought was so absurd that she barely restrained herself from laughing. "Can a husband steal from his own wife anyway?"

"Maybe not in the eyes of the law, depending on how you had your business set up, but that doesn't mean he couldn't have hidden money that you were unaware of."

She shook her head. She felt dizzy, and she wrapped her arms around herself, like she could ward off Ash's wild claims. *Not William. There's no way. He never would've betrayed me like that.*

"That's not possible," she whispered. "William wasn't

perfect, but he wasn't a thief. He loved me. Why would you even suggest such a thing?"

Ash held up his hands. "I'm sorry. I shouldn't have even suggested it since I have no proof. It must have been one of the bookkeepers." He pulled out his phone and began texting someone. "Let me contact my brother Phin. He's a lawyer. He's not in business law or marriage law, but hey, he'll at least know who to talk to, if all else fails."

Violet felt like someone had shoved her underwater, and she couldn't swim fast enough to the surface. The water was thick, viscous, and she felt it pulling her down, down, down. Panic settled inside her chest. She couldn't push the thought of William stealing from her out of her head, no matter if there wasn't any proof that he'd committed a crime.

He wouldn't have. There's no way. He was a good guy. Our marriage was happy and normal, and it had its problems, but don't all marriages?

"Wait," she said to Ash. He looked up in surprise. "Please don't text your brother about this. I need to think."

Ash blinked. "I just sent the text. Shit." He leaned toward her, his forehead creasing. "Violet, are you okay? You look really pale."

Hearing that he'd already sent the text made Violet want to shrivel up and die from embarrassment. She should never have asked Ash for help, she thought in a panic. She should've filed for bankruptcy and let the business go. William had always told her that it wouldn't end well. *You aren't good with numbers. How can you run a business if you're bad at something so important?*

Ash put his laptop away and took her hand, which she realized was shaking. "We'll figure this out," he said in a low voice. "When I said I'd help you, I meant it. I don't know if we can save your business, but I'm going to try my hardest. I know how much it means to you."

She took a deep breath, then another. Eventually, her heart slowed; the panic began to recede. "Thank you," she whispered finally.

After that, they sat in silence, drinking their coffee. Ash seemed lost in thought, and Violet found herself studying his profile, much like she had done when she'd first seen him at the Fainting Goat a month ago. It was silly, but watching him like this calmed her nerves somehow. Maybe because he looked so capable, so strong. Like he could handle anything the world threw at him.

In the sunlight pouring through the bakery's windows, his handsomeness was only magnified. To her delight, his hair sparkled in the sunlight, the light bringing out the red in the strawberry-blond strands. A light dusting of a beard dotted his cheeks and jaw.

"What color is your beard?" she asked abruptly.

He blinked before laughing. "Um, it's kind of reddish blond? But it's patchy and doesn't grow in very well, so I always shave it. Why?"

"No reason. I like you clean-shaven. It shows off your jaw nicely."

His teeth flashed white as he smiled. "Is that a compli ment? I can't believe it. I thought we were platonic business associates now."

"Don't push your luck. And anyway, that doesn't mean I can't admire my business associate from afar. I'm not blind."

"Neither am I." His gaze traveled from her breasts to her face, and Violet felt that gaze like a hand caressing her. "I have to say, you're the most beautiful business associate I've ever seen."

She laughed. "You're shameless."

"I know, but you like it." He leaned so close that his breath ruffled her hair. "I can't stop thinking about you, you know. How you looked when I was inside you. The way you said my name when you came."

Violet's blood heated until it boiled. The entire bakery faded away, and it was as if they were the only two people in existence. She closed her eyes, her own memories flooding back to her.

Why do I keep saying no? It doesn't have to be serious. God knows he knows his way around a woman's body.

Violet had the sudden urge to give in a second time, but when William's face appeared in her mind, she shook her head. Disgust replaced desire. Where had the staid, boring Violet gone? How had she transformed into this person she hardly recognized? A person who had one-night stands. A person who had forgotten all about the man she'd loved and lost, like he'd never existed.

"I should head home," she said as she rose from the table, almost knocking the chair to the floor. Grabbing her coffee, she didn't stop to hear Ash's protest. When she heard footsteps behind her, she just picked up her pace.

"Dammit, Violet." He grabbed her arm and turned her toward him. "How many times are you going to do this? Run away from the obvious?"

Her face turned hot. "I'm not running away. I'm leaving what is obviously a situation that's not good for me. Or for you, for that matter."

"Why? I want the exact reasons why I shouldn't throw you over my shoulder, take you home, and fuck you until you're hoarse from screaming my name." He crowded her until her back was against her car. "Because unless you give me a good reason or five, I'll know for sure that you're just running away."

She shivered, but not from fear: the intensity in Ash's gaze only sparked her own desire for him. She wanted him to take her back to his place and fuck her. God, she wanted that. She wanted it so intensely that she couldn't find the words to tell him that this was all a bad idea.

"It doesn't matter how much I want you," she said softly. His gaze heated at her words, but she shook her head. "I do want you. You know that. That doesn't mean it won't end badly for us both. Just because I want to eat an entire pan of brownies doesn't mean it won't make me sick later."

"I'm not a pan of brownies, although I appreciate the comparison all the same." He twirled a strand of her hair around his finger. "If I can't have you in my bed again, then let me take you out. Remember that date you agreed to go on with me?"

Violet knew she'd been well and truly caught. In that

moment, with Ash touching her and with the heat of his body pressed against her, she felt her defenses fall to pieces. What was one date? It wasn't a commitment. It wasn't even sex. Just food and conversation.

You keep telling yourself that.

"Fine, one date. Just one." At his elated expression, she poked him in the chest. "No shenanigans."

"Oh, I promise. I'll be on my best behavior." He stepped away from her with a wry smile. "See? I can behave myself."

She hated that her first thought was that she wished he *wouldn't* behave himself. *I'm an idiot.*

Violet had never felt so torn in her life. She'd always thought of herself as a rational person, but when it came to Ash, all rationality disappeared. He was like a magnet, drawing her closer and closer to him, no matter how hard she tried to push him away.

She shouldn't move closer to him. She should let him go home, let them both cool off. And yet she'd yearned for him so intensely that she found herself placing her hand on his chest over his thumping heart, their gazes locked. He took a deep breath, but he didn't touch her again.

I could fall in love with him. That stray thought both excited and terrified her. Her fingers dug into the fabric of his shirt.

He cupped her cheek, and when she tipped her head back, she could only feel sheer elation when he kissed her. It was like fireworks bursting across her skin. He tasted like coffee, his mouth heated, the scruff of his beard providing a delicious contrast to his soft lips. He kissed her like he'd seduced her: thoroughly, slowly. She didn't care that they were in a parking lot in the middle of the day. She didn't care about anything except that this kiss was turning her inside out.

"I should go," she whispered, although it was half-hearted. "Text me where you want to go on our date."

Ash didn't say anything. He kissed her forehead, her temples. Violet took in a shuddered breath. How could she say no to a man who kissed her like that?

Seeing him in her rearview mirror as she drove away, she had a distinct feeling that she wouldn't be able to resist him much longer, even with the knowledge that he'd most likely break her heart.

*a*sh was on pins and needles for the weekend to arrive. It didn't help that Trent had asked him to finish up some financial statements that week, and Ash had had to put aside thinking about Violet to finish the job. Trent had seemed to sense that Ash's mind was elsewhere, but he'd thankfully kept his big mouth shut.

Twenty-four hours before their date, Ash texted Violet. *I don't want to just take you to dinner. I want to take you somewhere else.*

Like the playground? she replied with a winky-face emoji.

Better than that. Can I pick you up around ten tomorrow morning?

Now I'm curious enough to say yes.

Despite Violet's best efforts, Ash wouldn't tell her where he was taking her. He hoped this mad scheme he'd concocted would work. He wanted to take Violet away from Fair Haven, and away from everything that was holding her back. He knew that her business's financial issues, along with being reminded of her husband while living with her mother-in-law, were causing her to push him away.

The next morning as he drove them to their destination, he glanced over at her. She seemed more relaxed today, a smile playing about her lips. Large sunglasses framed her face, and earrings that sparkled green in the sunlight hung to her shoulders. Whenever she caught him looking at her, she would laugh and blush.

Maybe I could have something real. Something like love. It was a dangerous thought. What had happened to his resolve never to fall in love? With Violet, it was crumbling to pieces, and he almost couldn't regret it. He wanted to convince her that she didn't have to be afraid if she was with him. He would always take care of her. If he could, he would do everything in his power so she never had to worry about creditors knocking on her door, or anything else that life would try to throw at her.

Ash had never wanted to protect someone like he wanted to protect Violet. He once again wondered what the hell had been wrong with her husband. Had William loved her like she deserved to be loved? Ash wasn't convinced that he had. Then again, his opinion was only slightly biased.

When Ash exited the highway, it was only a few miles before Violet let out a surprised gasp when the fields came into view. Fields and fields of tulips covered the landscape, the colors a rainbow of hues. Ash had only seen the Skagit

County tulips once, and he'd been too young to appreciate them.

Now, he could appreciate them through Violet's sheer delight.

"Oh, this is amazing. I've always wanted to see the tulips but just never got around to it." She sighed happily. "They're so beautiful."

Ash thought that the most beautiful thing was her, in all honesty. After they found a parking spot—the area was fairly crowded and filled with both tourists and locals enjoying the sights—Violet grabbed Ash's arm with a bright smile on her face.

They followed the crowd of people at first, and Ash vaguely listened to one of the employees talk about how they grew the tulips. Violet pointed to a row of purple tulips. "Those are my favorite."

"The violet ones? I'm shocked," he teased.

"I'm nothing if not boring. Come on. Let's walk."

Ash wasn't about to protest. He and Violet walked along the road, Violet sometimes kneeling down to touch a tulip. She tried smelling a few, laughing when she realized that the tulips didn't have much of a smell. The sun shone down, the clouds even parting as the afternoon progressed. Although it was mid-April, it was a surprisingly warm day. Ash couldn't have planned it better.

Soon they found themselves mostly alone. Ash couldn't stop watching Violet: the way she tilted her head back and soaked in the sun's rays; the way she picked up a stray tulip that had already been cut and put it behind her ear; the way she smiled up at him and held on to his arm. Her hair sparkled in the sunlight, her cheeks rosy. She looked so alive, so happy, that Ash felt his heart twist in his chest.

I think I'm falling in love with her. I think I might have fallen for her the first time I saw her.

The feeling was rather like being plunged into a cold lake. At first, he couldn't breathe, and he struggled to regain his bearings. The world tilted on its axis; his feet seemed like they were full of cement. And then he surfaced and gasped, and suddenly it all just made sense.

Violet made sense.

She found another stray tulip on the ground. "Here's one for you," she said as she reached up to place it behind his ear. "Oh, you look very dashing like that."

His throat closed. He wanted to tell her how he felt, but something held him back. *I don't want to scare her*, he reasoned. Or perhaps he just didn't want to scare himself.

Overwhelmed with the realization that he loved her, he kissed her, right in the middle of the wide-open tulip fields, the sun heating his neck. Violet let out a little gasp of surprise before she melted against him. She twined her arms around his neck as he deepened the kiss. God, he wanted her. He'd wanted her for weeks now, and he didn't know if he would survive if she said no to him again.

Ash licked inside her mouth, his hands roving down her spine until he could squeeze her ass. Violet moaned, the sound of it making him hard.

"I want you, Violet," he admitted as he kissed her throat. "I haven't stopped wanting you."

She didn't push him away, thank God. She nodded, sighing, her breath ruffling his hair. "Me too. I'm tired of trying to deny it. God knows I can't resist you."

He thrilled at her words. The only reason he didn't take her right here in the fields was because they weren't truly alone—right then, a group of people came over the hill and started walking toward them. And it would be a bit uncomfortable on the hard ground, his rapidly diminishing logical side said.

Jittery with desire, he tried desperately to think. He didn't want to drive them back to Fair Haven before he could touch her. But if he had to wait, he would survive. He would wait an eternity for her.

Violet looked up at him through her dark lashes, waiting for the group of tourists to walk past them.

"I saw an inn as we were driving in. It said it had vacancies." She licked her lips.

It took a second for Ash's mind to make the connection. *Inn. Vacancy. Bed.* "Let's go."

They practically ran back to his car, Violet laughing when Ash almost ran into a man wearing a fanny pack and a straw hat. "Hey, watch where you're going!" the man yelled.

"Sorry!" Ash yelled back, and Violet just laughed harder.

He drove back down the road where they'd come. Waiting for the front desk clerk to swipe his credit card and give him the room key cards was the longest ten minutes of Ash's damn life. It didn't help that Violet kept touching him and pressing up against him like a cat in heat. He was so hard it was like someone had shoved an iron bar into his jeans.

"Would you like a menu for room service?" the clerk asked in a bored tone.

"No. We're fine. Just need the keys," Ash barked.

Violet pinched his ass and he glared at her. She just smiled innocently.

"There's a continental breakfast that starts at six a.m., and—"

"The keys. Please," said Ash.

The clerk frowned and, after swiping the key cards, handed them to Ash. "Have a nice stay."

He and Violet rushed upstairs. To Ash's consternation, the room key decided not to work. Ash swore long and low when the door beeped red after the third try.

Violet chortled. "Give it to me." She put the key card in the slot, waited, and pulled it out slowly. Green light. *Fucking finally.*

He shut the door behind them and pulled her into his arms. "You're mine," he growled. "You're all mine tonight."

She took the tulip from behind his ear, which he'd forgotten he'd still been wearing. He laughed and plucked the tulip from Violet's hair before kissing her. He kissed her for a long moment, savoring her. Then he took a step back.

"I want to see you. Show me everything I've been missing these past few weeks."

Violet's eyes gleamed. "Only if you do the same for me."

"Fine with me. Now," he said with a wolfish smile, "strip for me."

～

VIOLET SHIVERED at the look in Ash's eyes. Had anyone ever looked at her like that? With such sheer desire? Her heartbeat increased as she grasped the hem of her shirt and slowly pulled it off. She still wore a camisole, but the way Ash was gazing at her made her feel like she was already nude.

He sat down on the bed. "Keep going," he instructed. "Take your time."

Violet had never performed a striptease in her life, and she would've thought she would be too self-conscious to manage it. Right now, though, she felt infinitely sexy, and Ash watching her only emboldened her further. She stared into his eyes as she pushed one strap of her camisole down her shoulder, so slowly that Ash's jaw tightened.

She pushed the other strap down and pulled the camisole down about an inch to reveal the edges of her lacy bra. Her breasts ached, her nipples already hardened, and when she brushed her palm across one turgid peak, she gasped.

"Play with yourself. God, Violet, you're gorgeous."

She pushed her camisole down until it circled her hips, the

cool air of the inn room making goose bumps rise on her skin. She palmed one of her breasts before tweaking her nipple, the sensation causing her sex to clench with anticipation. A flush had crawled up Ash's cheeks. His eyes were hooded as he leaned back on the bed. He looked like a lazy cat stretching out in the sun, with his red-gold hair and predatory air.

"Do you want to see me?" Her voice was hoarse. "Or should I keep my bra on?" As she said the words, she cupped her breast beneath the lace cup of her bra. She rubbed her nipple and pinched it. All the while, she only watched Ash for his reaction.

"Fuck," he growled. "You tease." He reached out and snaked an arm around her waist, bringing her between his thighs. He buried his face between her breasts, kissing them and sucking at the soft skin. Violet tugged at his hair and ran her fingers through the silken strands.

Ash reached behind her and unhooked her bra. She laughed softly. So much for watching her undress herself. With a quick movement, he took off her bra and soon had one nipple in his mouth. He sucked with a pressure that made Violet's toes curl.

He lavished attention on her breasts until Violet's knees felt like jelly. She grasped his shoulders to keep from collapsing at his feet.

"I thought you wanted me to strip for you," she gasped out when he laved the other nipple.

"I couldn't resist putting my mouth on these beauties." He grinned up at her. "I love your breasts. I love how your nipples turn ruby-red when I suck them, and how you blush from your chest to your cheeks."

She pushed at him playfully. "Now you're being rude. Never comment on a woman's blush." Standing a foot away from him now, she took off her camisole and tossed it at him. He just inhaled the fabric's scent before discarding it.

"Take off your jeans. Now. Before I do it myself," he growled.

She clucked her tongue as she unbuttoned her pants and slowly slid them down her legs. She toed off her boots, making sure to bend down so Ash could get an eyeful of her breasts. When she heard him swear under his breath, she smiled.

When she stripped out of her panties and stood before him, completely nude, she let his gaze travel up her body, from her toes to her sex, to her breasts and then to her face. He reached out to embrace her, but she moved away from him before he could catch her.

"Uh-uh, it's your turn. Strip for me." Violet pulled on his arm before she sat down on the bed, making a point to lean backward so her breasts pointed upward, her legs parted slightly.

He shook his head. "You make a hard bargain," he joked, which made her roll her eyes and laugh. "But a promise is a promise."

He took off his shoes and socks in such an exaggerated manner that Violet started giggling. When he got to his shirt, he started undulating like some burlesque dancer who had also had too much to drink. Violet wolf-whistled when he tossed his shirt at her before touching his nipples and moaning loudly.

"Oh my God, stop! You're killing me!" she said through giggles.

She just kept laughing when he got to his jeans and almost fell on his face trying to dance and take them off at the same time. Breathless and red-faced, her eyes watering, she almost missed when he took off his boxers. Thank God she didn't, though. Seeing his hard cock unveiled, she felt her body tighten with desire, her laughter dying in her throat.

As he walked up to her, she curled her hand around his cock and squeezed. His jaw tightened. As he grew harder, she stared up at him and stroked him, making sure to squeeze him each time. A pearl of fluid leaked from the tip. She swirled her tongue around that tip; he groaned in response.

Violet took him into her mouth, loving the saltiness that coated her tongue. She couldn't take all of him, but with each bob of her head and swirl of her tongue, she felt his fingers tighten in her hair. She hadn't realized how powerful she could feel with a man like this in her thrall.

"Shit, Violet. Stop. You're going to make me come." Ash tugged on her hair, and she reluctantly let him go. But soon she forgot everything else when he pulled her toward the end of the bed, parted her thighs, and kneeled between them. He licked her sex right then. In relentless strokes, he tortured her, his mouth driving her wild.

Violet undulated against his lips, needing more pressure, more, more, more. She pinched her nipples. She cried out his name. She'd transformed into this sex goddess who didn't care about anything except wanting Ash's mouth, his hands, his cock. God, she just wanted *him*.

He pushed a finger inside her tight sheath and then a second finger. When he kissed and sucked her clit in time with the thrusts of his fingers, she exploded like dynamite. She shouted to the ceiling, writhing and shivering, her body on fire. Ash drew out her orgasm like a master pianist. She couldn't find enough air; she couldn't even see clearly. She was only a bundle of sensations.

As Violet came down from her orgasm, she vaguely heard Ash rustling around before she heard a foil packet opening. Opening her eyes, she looked up to see Ash rolling a condom down his cock as he gazed at her with an expression she'd never seen before: it was almost like he was in pain, his eyes dark and his forehead furrowed. She wanted to smooth those furrows from his brow, but she couldn't move. She was jelly, her bones having melted.

In a quick movement, Ash turned her onto her stomach and had her get on her knees. In this position, she felt more exposed than she'd ever been in her life. It only heightened her desire. Ash kissed her spine and spanked one ass cheek, making her yelp.

"I'm going to fuck you now, Violet," he said, the words like red silk around her senses. She shivered. "Are you ready for me?"

"Yes, please. I need you." She pushed her ass against

him. She needed him inside her so badly it was like an ache in her very soul.

With painful slowness, he thrust into her, filling her until she was sure she couldn't take another inch. She collapsed onto her arms, her fingers digging into the bedspread.

"God, you're tight. So beautiful. I couldn't stop thinking of you, dreaming of you." He punctuated each word with a thrust. His fingers dug into her hips as he fucked her, filling her in endless strokes. "The first second I saw you that night, I wanted you."

I felt the same. It was like there was no one else but you since. She wished she had the courage to say the words aloud, but for now, she kept them inside and close to her heart.

Ash pounded into her as he picked up his pace. Violet groaned and cried out, not caring that the people next door could surely hear them. The headboard knocked against the wall and the bed squeaked under her. If she hadn't been so caught up in the moment, she would've laughed at all the noise they were making.

Ash began rubbing her clit, the movement of his thumb in tandem with his thrusts like before. Violet bit her lip, tasting blood, as her belly tensed. Her orgasm built. When she fell off the precipice a second time, she was fairly certain she wouldn't survive it. She gasped in a strangled breath, her entire body quaking.

Ash shouted his release. He gripped her hips to keep her still as he filled her, and the scent of salt and sex in the air was like a heady, intoxicating perfume. Violet felt dizzy.

She was glad she was already lying on her stomach, or she would've collapsed, her limbs completely useless.

I'm dead; he's killed me. And what a way to go.

Violet heard water running. Ash murmured something and then a blanket covered her. Ash then got in bed and spooned behind her, and the warmth of his body and sound of his beating heart lulled her into a dreamless sleep.

13

*V*iolet licked her fingers and sighed happily. "That was the best continental breakfast I've ever eaten," she declared. "The Fruit Loops were a particular delight."

Ash smiled wryly. "Don't try the coffee, then. You might be disappointed." He grimaced as he drank his own cup of coffee before setting it aside. "I need real coffee. Do you want some? I'm dying."

Violet kissed him, letting the sheet she'd wrapped around herself fall to her lap. They'd woken at dawn to make love a second time before falling back asleep. A few hours later, starving and caffeine-deprived, they'd snagged a few bagels, mini boxes of cereal, and milk cartons from the continental breakfast just minutes before it had ended.

"I don't want you to go anywhere," she said. "Coffee isn't that important."

"It's pretty important, but with breasts like yours..." Ash kissed her neck as he fondled her breasts, making her shiver. "You'd make a man forget his own name with tits this pretty."

She pinched him. "Don't be vulgar." She said it with a giggle, then a sigh, as he licked her neck before sucking on the skin of her collarbone. "Thank you for bringing me here. I needed to get away."

He wrapped an arm around her; she snuggled against him.

"You're welcome. I didn't plan on staying the night, if you're curious," he said.

"Oh really? You had planned to just look at a bunch of flowers and then drive me home while keeping your hands to yourself?"

He laughed. "Okay, fine. I'd *hoped*. But I didn't expect it."

"I expected it," she said, making him laugh again.

She listened to his heart thump with her ear on his chest. Rain started to fall, pattering against the window. Violet felt like they were in their own little cocoon, safe from the world outside. She never wanted to leave this bed or this room. She didn't even care that the bed squeaked terribly or that the coffee apparently tasted like dishwater. It was the best hotel room she'd ever stayed in because she was here with Ash.

It'd been so long since Violet had felt protected. Cherished. Wanted. After William's death, her life had been one disaster after another, and although she'd hoped that moving in with Martha would help get her life back on track, things had only snowballed instead. Yet Ash had shown up and had somehow been the one thing—the one person—she'd been searching for.

Ash made it extremely difficult *not* to love him. Underneath his devil-may-care exterior and playboy habits, he was caring and thoughtful. She had a feeling that he'd been searching for something, too, and hadn't found it in the arms of the many women he'd slept with. That thought nipped at her, jealousy blooming inside her. It was silly, being jealous of women who had known him before Violet had met him, but there it was. Sometimes emotions were irrational like that.

"You're very quiet," said Ash, breaking Violet's train of thought. "Anything wrong?"

She smiled. How did he know her moods so easily? He was definitely one in a million. William had never been all that interested in talking about his feelings or his worries, and he hadn't usually noticed when something had been eating at Violet.

"Nothing's wrong. I'm just thinking," she replied.

"About what?" He brushed her hair from her forehead with gentle fingers.

"Tell me something about you that no one else knows."

"Oh, that's what you're thinking about? You want to know all my dirty secrets?"

She grinned. "I'd already assumed they were dirty."

He laughed. "Okay, ask away."

Violet thought for a long moment. "What's your middle

name?" At his groan, she knew she'd landed on something good. "Now you're definitely going to have to tell me. Come on, spill."

Disgruntled, he said, "My real name isn't Ash. It's a nickname."

"Go on."

"My mom had terrible taste in names. All of my siblings have stupid names."

"That's great, but I want to know *yours*."

Ash groaned, pinched his nose, and then finally said, "Ashley Nigel Stuart Younger. There. That's my full name. Happy?"

Violet's lips twitched. Ash's real name was *Ashley?* At that, Violet burst out laughing, more so at his obvious discomfiture than because it was a truly terrible name.

"Yeah, yeah, laugh away. And if you tell anybody, you'll regret it."

She forced herself to stop laughing, but when she thought of his middle names, the laughter bubbled over again. "I'm sorry," she gasped, "it's not even that funny. It's just the look on your face."

Growling, he started to tickle her. She had to beg for mercy for him to stop.

"Your turn," he said, his eyes sparkling. "What's your middle name?"

"Ann. Sorry. It's a pretty standard middle name."

"Then tell me something no one else knows about you." Ash crossed his arms, waiting.

Violet had to wrack her brain for a moment to find a

secret to tell. She was, sadly, not one of those people with a colorful past. "I hate hamsters. One bit me when I was in first grade, and to this day I can't look at one without getting freaked out."

"Hamsters? Really?"

"Yes, really." She threw a pillow at his amused face, and he grunted. "They're creepy. They're only awake at night, too, and they eat their young! No hamsters." She shuddered.

"I promise I won't get you one, then. Although I've been thinking I should get you a fish. You know, so if you need to use that excuse again, you don't have to lie."

After that, they wrestled and tickled each other, forcing each other to tell random secrets about each other. Ash hated tuna fish; Violet could eat an entire jar of pickles in one sitting. Ash had been stung by a jellyfish as a kid and Trent had peed on his leg (it hadn't helped); Violet had shaved her sister Vera's eyebrow in her sleep and had been grounded for a month as a result. Ash liked to watch the cooking channel; Violet did too, especially the one where the contestants had to put together dishes with random, terrible ingredients.

They fell silent, simply enjoying each other's company. Eventually, Ash pushed Violet's hair from her forehead and asked, "Penny for your thoughts?"

"Oh, everything, nothing. I was thinking about how a month ago I had just moved to a new town and was running away from everything, and now I'm here, with you. How two years ago I was burying my husband."

"Do you miss him?"

Violet sighed. "I do miss him. Every day. But each day it gets easier."

"I'm sorry."

"But I think what's worse, in a way, is that I don't think about him as much as I used to. I'll always miss him, but more and more I feel like there's room for something else. Someone else."

Ash's gaze darkened. "I'm glad."

The words floated on her tongue, but she didn't have the courage right then to say them. *Soon. I just need more time. It's too quick, right? How can I have fallen in love with someone after only knowing him a month?*

"The last time I saw William, we fought." When Ash didn't say anything, she kept talking. Maybe she couldn't say the words *I love you*, but she could talk about this. She needed to talk about it for some reason she didn't understand.

"He was angry about my business. The money wasn't coming in and things were a mess. He was pissed because I had focused on the business so much that I'd neglected our marriage. If I wasn't up all night making jewelry, I was working on inventory and my website and emails during the day. William had to fend for himself."

"Where did he work?"

"He was an engineer. He liked his job, but it was stressful. When I'd started my business, his job kept changing. His company kept laying people off, and the only way William kept his job was to be downgraded or moved. It was stressful, to say the least. Then coming home to me stressing about my business only made things worse. I thought that I could help make us more money to ease his burden.

"The day he died, we got into a huge fight." Violet took in a shaky breath. "I was angry with him because he'd never supported my dream. Not really. He'd made me agree to let him do the books because he knew I was bad with money. But apparently it didn't make a difference, did it?"

Ash stroked her hair. "I'm sorry," he said again.

"Don't be sorry. It was my own fault. I was selfish. I was so focused on being successful that I didn't care about my marriage or William. I even told him that I wanted to end things. He left…and never came home."

Guilt choked her then—guilt, grief, misery. She missed William, but most of all, she missed the William she'd married and fallen in love with. If she hadn't been so self-ish, William wouldn't have gotten angry and gotten into his car. He wouldn't have driven out into the pouring rain, he wouldn't have been at the stoplight when that driver had decided texting was more important than paying attention. He wouldn't have slammed into William's car.

"I should've stopped him," she whispered. "I should've told him that he mattered more than some stupid business. I cared more about my pride than I did about him, and he paid for it with his life."

Ash shifted against her. "Jesus, Violet, you can't blame yourself. It was an accident that could've happened to anyone. If you should blame anyone, blame the driver who hit him. Was he drunk?"

"No, just texting. So stupid, right? One second he wasn't paying attention. The next, he'd slammed into the driver's side of William's car so hard that he was killed on impact. The driver survived."

"Don't they always," said Ash, his voice grim.

"I know it doesn't make sense. I know that others were at fault. But if I had known, I could've prevented it from happening. And I hate that our last words were ones of anger. I'll have to live with that for the rest of my life."

Ash held her close, and she let herself be comforted by his presence and his arms around her. She hadn't let herself feel protected in far too long.

"When I was a kid," Ash said quietly after a while, "I watched my brother Trent blame himself for our mom. He was the oldest, and I think he took on a parental role with all of us as a result. When our mom died, he took it hard. Probably harder than I did." He laughed, but it was a hollow sound. "I was weirdly glad that she wasn't suffering anymore, or dragging us all down with it."

"What happened to your mom?" asked Violet.

"She killed herself."

He said the words tonelessly, and he felt Violet flinch against him. He didn't feel anything, saying those words.

He hadn't felt anything about his mother—or his father—for a long, long time.

She touched his cheek. "Oh, Ash, I'm so sorry. Do you want to talk about it?"

"Not really, but then again, I did bring it up." He pressed a kiss to her temple, inhaling the scent of her hair. "I didn't bring it up to make you sad, so much as to tell you that you can't blame yourself for other people's choices. Trent thought he could save our mom, and when he didn't, it tore him apart. He almost lost Lizzie and his daughter because of it. Seeing that convinced me that I wouldn't let myself be dragged down by other people."

He realized how harsh that sounded, but it was true. His parents' marriage had been turbulent and messy; they'd loved each other in a way that had brought out the worst in them both. His father, Edward, had been a proud man who had seen his own dreams fall apart, and with his wife, Beatrice, suffering from severe mental illness that had only worsened, it had been a whirlpool of abuse and rage that Ash and his siblings had all been caught up in.

Ash knew that his parents hadn't always been so screwed up. He vaguely remembered happier times, when there had been laughter in their house. But as his father's anger had increased, his mother had started to disintegrate. She had begun to take pills to numb the pain.

Ash remembered one instance when he'd been seven years old. He'd arrived home from a friend's house to find Phin and Lucy outside, even though it was already dark and cold. Phin was only five, and Lucy was three. There was no one around to watch them, not even Trent or Thea. Ash was young, but old enough to know his siblings shouldn't be outside.

"We need to go inside," said Ash. He took Lucy's hand, but she refused to budge.

"Dad said we had to stay out here." Phin pushed his glasses up his nose, the frames way too big for him. Small and pale, Phin hadn't made any friends in kindergarten and preferred to sit and read a book on the playground. It didn't help that he was already reading at a fourth-grade level when the rest of his class was still working on the alphabet.

Ash frowned. "It's dark out. Come on, you must've heard wrong. Let's go."

Lucy started crying when Ash hauled her up. "I want to play! I want to play!" she cried as she wriggled away from her brother. "You're not my mom!"

Ash heard a yell from the house. Going to the living room window, he peeked through the small opening between the curtains to see his parents standing in the middle of the room. His dad's face was red; his mom was crying. Ash watched in confusion, wondering what was happening, when his dad took his mom's arm and shook her like a dog with a rat.

Ash cried out, but he slapped a hand over his mouth and ducked down when his dad swiveled toward the window. Ash heard another sound, something like a slap, before he crawled back to his siblings.

Phin was shivering, but Lucy was still intent on playing

with her dolls. Ash picked up Lucy and one of her dolls, covering her mouth to keep her quiet.

"Come on," he hissed at Phin. "We need to go."

Hours later, Trent found them in the woods a house away. Even though he was only eleven, Trent acted like a kid much older. When Trent found them, Ash would never forget the look of relief on his brother's face.

Ash had known, even at seven, that something had changed between his parents and that things would never be the same again.

He'd been right.

"My mom overdosed on purpose when I was eleven," said Ash to Violet. "I came home to find her dead. Trent was a zombie, Thea was crying, and there I was, relieved. Phin and Lucy were too young to really understand, although I think Phin understood more than he let on."

The memories haunted him to this day, and sometimes they came upon him at the oddest times. Right then, he pushed the memories away before they pulled him under again.

"And your dad?" Violet asked.

"He turned into a mean asshole, and nobody was sad when he died. Depressing, right?" He set his chin on top of Violet's head. "I guess I should've warned you that I come from a fucked-up family."

She patted his forearm. "Not one person in the universe doesn't have baggage. Not unless they're a newborn, and even then, they probably have at least an issue or two." She tilted her head back to look up at him. "Although I can't say that my parents were terrible. They were actually pretty great."

"Good, somebody should have nice parents. Where are they now?"

"Traveling around the country in their RV. My dad retired from the military, and a month later they sold their house, bought an RV, and started their new adventure. I think they're in Arizona right now, if I remember correctly. My dad thinks the Pacific Northwest is too cold in the winter, so they usually stay down south during the rainy months."

"I can't blame them there. Every year I dread the rain and think I should move, and every year I stay put and suck it up."

"Sounds like a true Pacific Northwesterner."

Ash had never talked to anyone as truthfully as he had to Violet. That spark that had begun when he'd first met her only grew. Seeing her amongst the tulips yesterday had shown him how much he wanted her. Now, their conversation had only cemented that fact. He'd never felt as comfortable or safe with someone else as he had with her. He'd never admit it, though. A man had his pride.

"I know we're both fucked up," he began. He laughed a little at that intro. "But what I said last night was true: I never stopped thinking about you. You make me want things I never thought I'd want."

"Really?" Her eyes were wide.

"Yes. I want to try, Violet. I want to see if we can make

this real." He squeezed her hand. "How about it? It doesn't have to be forever. But just for now."

When she didn't reply for a long moment, he wondered if he'd overstepped. Terrified that she was about to reject him, he said, "You don't have to answer now——"

"No—I mean, my answer is yes. I want that, too. It's scary and part of me would like to run away, but I'm trying not to give in to that part of me." Her eyes shone as she gazed up at him. "I want to try with you, too."

He kissed her, and then he was pushing her back onto the bed and climbing on top of her. She wrapped her arms and her legs around him, her sweet softness enveloping him completely. All thoughts of parents, of bad memories, of their longings and fears, all dissipated when he held her in his arms.

Afterward, they were both starving again and went to find lunch. The rain had stopped, but it was still misty and gray. Discovering a cafe not far from the tulip fields, they sat together in a cozy booth that provided some modicum of privacy, eating and talking and laughing.

"Why did you make me this?" Ash asked as he pulled out the bracelet Violet had left on his pillow. "You never said why."

She shrugged, her cheeks a little red. "It was stupid, but it was like I didn't want you to forget me."

"Even as you sneaked out of my apartment without saying goodbye?"

"I never said it made sense."

He rubbed one of the beads. "I'd wear it, except it's too small."

"Really?" She took the bracelet and tried to fit it on his wrist. "Geez, you have huge arms! I should've known. Here, I'll fix it. Then you won't have any excuse not to wear it."

She began pulling out jewelry-making supplies from her bag like a magician, and to Ash's immense delight, the table was soon covered with beads, twine, hooks, pliers, scissors, and other tools he'd never seen in his life. Violet began to take apart the bracelet, her hands dexterous and sure, and Ash realized he could watch her create jewelry for hours if she'd let him.

"Can you show me how you make jewelry?" he asked. At her surprised look, he shrugged. "I'm curious."

"Well, of course I can show you. It's not every day that I get to teach a manly man like yourself how to make jewelry."

He chuckled. "I'm equal opportunity for accessories. Now, how the hell did you get the charms on anyway?"

They spent the rest of the afternoon at that booth, Ash putting together a very ugly bracelet while Violet redid the one she'd made him. An hour later, she had him hold out his wrist so she could tie the bracelet around it: now it fit perfectly.

"Excellent." She smiled when he held it up to the light. "Tiger's eye looks good on you."

It wasn't exactly something Ash would wear, but it wasn't feminine, either. Besides, he had a feeling that if she'd made him a bright pink necklace covered in flowers, he'd wear it for her, he was that far gone.

He tied the bracelet he'd created for her onto her wrist. "Fair is fair."

"I'll never take it off," she said, and Ash had a feeling she meant it.

14

*A*sh had a pile of things he needed to do today, but he couldn't stop thinking about Violet's books. He'd gone over the spreadsheets, the receipts, the bank statements—all of it. The numbers on the bank statements and spreadsheets didn't add up, yet Ash couldn't figure out why. Tired and frustrated, he'd gone to bed well after three in the morning Sunday night.

When he'd gotten into the office this morning, he'd begun calling the bookkeepers who'd helped with Violet's books. One had resulted in a disconnected number. The second had been sent to a voicemail that might have been the wrong number entirely. The third had been the voice-mail of an actual bookkeeper, but Ash hadn't had high hopes that Jeffrey Martin, CPA, would return his rather odd phone call anytime soon.

With only a few hours of sleep, he was tired and

grumpy. He was tempted to go home early. Although Trent was technically his boss, he wasn't a hard-ass about Ash being in the office, either. Trent worked at all three restaurant locations in some capacity, although his main office was here at the Fainting Goat, along with Ash's. But owning and running restaurants wasn't done by sitting behind a desk. More often than not, Trent was on the front lines.

Ash hadn't seen Trent today, and for that, he was grateful. He didn't need his brother's questions about why Ash had bags under his eyes or was bleary-eyed. Picking up the latest financial statement for Trent's tapas restaurant, La Bonita, Ash focused on the business at hand, shoving everything related to Violet to the back of his mind.

After their weekend together, Ash had returned to Fair Haven certain that he and Violet would make a go of things. He'd worried that she would freak out and decide she wasn't ready for anything serious, but to his relief, she had been the happiest he'd ever seen her. The drive back to Fair Haven had been full of conversation and laughter. Ash had stopped on the side of the road more than once to kiss Violet and make her blush scarlet. He'd teased her that she should've been named Scarlet instead of Violet, which had earned him an eye roll.

Ash was finishing up this last document when he glanced at one of the Fainting Goat's bank statements. There was nothing on there that gave him any cause for alarm: food purchases, supplies, credit card payments—

Credit cards. Why hadn't he thought of that? He'd seen a number of credit card payments on Violet's bank statements, but he'd thought nothing of them. What business didn't have a credit card or two? But something niggled at him regardless. Maybe it was intuition, or maybe it was exhaustion. He just knew he needed to look more closely in that direction.

Pushing the restaurants' paperwork aside, Ash pulled out Violet's file, which he kept in his briefcase whenever he came into work. He'd more often than not think of something to pursue, and knowing he wouldn't be able to concentrate on his actual work, he'd given in and made sure he had her documents on hand at all times.

He pulled the stack of bank statements from the folder, now in an orderly pile by date. Ash then began to highlight every instance of a credit card payment, and before long, the statements were a sea of yellow.

When he began looking through the documents, he realized there were no credit card statements or payments. He went through all the files on the jump drives—nothing. He blew out a frustrated breath. He'd have to talk to Violet about how he could access those statements. There was something about them that just didn't look right, and because he hadn't yet put his finger on why, it was going to bug him until he unraveled the mystery.

"Hey, do you have those financial statements?" Trent called as he walked by Ash's office. "Bring 'em to me if you do."

Ash had only finished half of them, but, preferring to get the interrogation over now, he went to Trent's office with the papers in hand.

"I didn't have time to finish all of them, but I'll have them done by tomorrow," he said.

Trent raised an eyebrow. "What else are you working on?"

"Some other project."

At Ash's evasive tone, Trent leaned back in his office chair and set his feet up on his desk. "Really? Like Violet Fielding?"

"You're as bad as Thea." Ash crossed his arms. "Maybe. Does it matter?"

"No. I'm not going to tell you who you can and cannot date." Trent snorted. "You're my brother, not my kid. Thank God." Trent suddenly paled. "Oh God, Bea will be dating eventually, won't she? I'll have to lock her up until she's thirty-five."

Ash sat down in a chair, laughing. "Good luck with that. You do know her mother, right? She'll have all the boys flocking around her."

"I'm not sure if you're complimenting or insulting my wife, but I'll take it as the former."

"Complimenting, definitely. I'm not insane."

"Hmm." Trent tapped his fingers on the desktop. "I might've heard through the grapevine that you and Violet left for the weekend."

"Christ, seriously? I hate small towns. I thought this wasn't any of your business?"

"It's not, except that you *are* my little brother, and I know that you've never gone on a weekend away with any woman. You prefer one night and one night only. I've seen how you've moved from one conquest to the next. I'm not judging you for it, by the way. But that doesn't mean I don't worry about you, either."

Ash wanted to die. He wanted to crawl under the desk and never come out again. Since their parents had been mostly useless, Trent had taken on the monumental task of being a parent-like figure to Ash and their other siblings. Even though all of them were now adults, things hadn't really changed in that regard. Ash felt rather like when he'd come home from fifth grade with a suspension notice and Trent had looked at him with such disappointment that Ash had felt terrible for weeks.

"I did take Violet somewhere," Ash admitted. "I hadn't planned on making a weekend of it, but things happened. I told her I wanted something more serious, and she felt the same."

"Really?" Trent's eyes widened. "How many times have you told me that you weren't meant for something serious?" Marveling, Trent shook his head, laughing a little. "Well, well, well. I guess with the right woman, anything is possible."

"Are you done yet? I need to finish something."

"About that—what project is this? Should I be worried that it'll affect your work here?"

Ash gritted his teeth. "No, it won't. I'm helping Violet out with her books, is all. They're a mess."

"And you're doing it for free? Damn. I've heard everything now. I have one question for you, though."

"Can I go after you ask it?"

"Sure. Do you love her?"

Ash swallowed, a lump forming in his throat. The question was like a sledgehammer to his brain. *Do I?* It was an easy enough question on the surface. Yes or no. But if he said yes, it would be like a promise he'd have to keep. Staring at his older brother, Ash found himself wanting to be honest when normally he would prevaricate.

What the hell has happened to me?

"I think I do." He pushed his fingers through his hair, disheveling it. "When did you know with Lizzie?"

Trent's expression took on a faraway look. "Probably when I couldn't stop thinking about her and missed her even when I didn't see her for a day. When you feel like you'll do anything you can for that person...that's how you know. Suddenly it's not all about you. It's about making someone else happy."

Ash's heart clenched, because Trent's words rang true. Ash wanted Violet to be happy, to feel safe, to feel loved. He wanted to take all of her worries and carry them for her. He didn't know when his feelings of lust had transformed into something more, but he'd be an idiot to act like they weren't there.

Terror mixed with elation inside him. Part of him wanted to go and tell Violet right then, while the other part of him knew that Violet would probably run in the opposite direction like a scared rabbit.

"I think Violet has more commitment issues than even me," said Ash wryly. "Hard to believe, right?"

"Take things slow. Don't push her too hard, but don't let

her cut you off because she's scared, either." Trent's eyes went sad. "I lost years with Lizzie because I was hurt and she was hurt. She pushed me away and I let her. Don't make the same mistake I did."

Knowing that Trent and Lizzie had spent almost a decade apart before reuniting, Ash knew his brother spoke the truth. Nodding, Ash returned to his own office and shut the door.

He needed to think. He needed to see Violet. He needed to figure out how the hell he was going to convince Violet that although her first love had died, that didn't mean she had died along with him.

When Ash began to gather his things to head home, his cell phone rang. He answered the call as he walked out to his car, and he almost dropped his phone when he realized it was Jeffrey Martin, the bookkeeper he'd called earlier.

"Thanks for returning my call," said Ash as he got inside his car. "I wanted to talk about a client you worked with about four years ago. A William Fielding? He was the husband of Violet Fielding, who owns White Dahlia Jewelry."

"Yes, I remember them both. I never really talked with Ms. Fielding, but I worked closely with Mr. Fielding. May I ask who you are in relation to them?"

"I'm Ash Younger. I'm also a CPA working on Ms. Fielding's books; she's authorized me to look into her accounts and track down former bookkeepers." The last part was a bit of a white lie that he hoped Violet would forgive. "I'm not sure if you're aware that Mr. Fielding passed away a couple of years ago?"

"I didn't. I'm sorry for Ms. Fielding's loss." Ash heard rustling before Jeffrey said, "Yes, now I remember more clearly. I only worked with them for three months before Mr. Fielding essentially told me I was no longer needed. You know how it goes."

"I wanted to ask if you know of any other bookkeepers the Fieldings employed that may have skimmed money from their accounts. There are large sums of money that are unaccounted for, and Violet—Ms. Fielding—is rather desperate to figure out where that money went."

Jeffrey was silent for a long moment, and Ash wondered if the call had been dropped.

"I'm not aware of any other bookkeepers skimming money," he finally replied, "but I did become aware that Mr. Fielding himself was funneling money to pay off non-business credit cards. When I asked him about it, he got defensive and told me to mind my business. After that, he let me go. I had just begun my CPA practice, and I was too worried about my own business to get into some messy tangle with him. Besides, I wasn't sure if he and his wife had some kind of arrangement. Marriage tends to make money matters murky."

Ash blew out a breath. He hadn't wanted to entertain the idea that William had been the one skimming money, but this seemed to prove it.

Goddammit, how am I going to tell Violet that her husband stole from her?

"Do you have any more information?" asked Ash, rather hoping Jeffrey said no.

"I don't. That's all I know. Best of luck, though. Things like this are never fun for anyone."

After hanging up, Ash groaned and thumped his head on the car headrest. He didn't have proof of Jeffrey's allegations yet, but it at least pointed him in a particular direction. If Ash could gather the evidence and figure out if William had been doing something underhanded, would Violet even believe Ash? It was one thing to find out that some random employee had stolen from you; it was entirely different to discover your spouse—the person you loved and trusted most in the world—had stolen from you—if that had even been the case here.

Can you send me your business's credit card statements? Ash texted Violet. *Preferably electronic ones?*

Let me look in my files, she replied. *I thought they'd be in the folder I gave you, but I guess not?*

About a half hour later, Ash's inbox pinged with an email from Violet with a number of attachments. Opening them, he saw that they were those credit card statements. His heartbeat sped up in excitement.

Bingo.

When Ash arrived home, he began to look through the credit card statements Violet had sent him. He compared them with the transactions he'd highlighted on the bank statements. Many of the transactions lined up with the credit card statements, but that certainly didn't prove that anything nefarious had been occurring. So

William hadn't included them on the spreadsheets. Maybe he'd forgotten, or they'd gotten lumped in with other transactions.

Growling, he was about to go to bed and start again in the morning when a book of checks fell out of the folder. He frowned. Had he looked through these? He began flipping through them, staring at the carbon copies until his bleary eyes could barely focus.

Violet's voice echoed in his head. *No, that's my handwriting. Did I mention that my handwriting is basically chicken scratch?*

Ash stared at the handwriting on the carbon copy, the text barely legible now. He realized that the *s* in *Eastern* was written as a cursive *s*, and suddenly, Ash was grabbing at the receipt that Violet had identified as one she'd written herself.

On the handwritten receipt, the lowercase *s* in *beads* was written not as a cursive *s* in this instance, but it was printed. Just like all of Violet's notes were written. Ash couldn't find any instance where she'd used a cursive lowercase *s* instead.

He began comparing the handwriting on the carbon copies of the checks and found more differences. They were subtle, and anyone just glancing at them would never have thought they weren't Violet's handwriting. But Ash knew in his gut right then that Violet hadn't written those checks: William had.

William had been forging checks from Violet's business to pay off credit cards he must've also taken out in her name. Considering that Violet had had no reason to distrust her husband, she'd never looked closely at the old checks or at credit card statements that were from the same companies where she'd opened legitimate credit cards.

"You bastard," Ash muttered. "You slimy, thieving bastard. How could you do that to your fucking wife?"

Ash wondered what William had been paying for. Hookers? Drugs? Both? Disgust radiating from him, he tossed the papers onto the coffee table.

He had his evidence. Considering the money had been used to pay off credit cards, Ash had no idea if that money could even be recovered. Worse, he would have to tell Violet, but first he needed to absolutely confirm it had been William's handwriting.

He couldn't just tell her about William and not help her. In the morning, Ash called all of the banks in town, praying that one would accept his application for a loan.

15

*V*iolet squinted as she was about to finish off the clasp for the bracelet she was making for Lizzie. Picking up her smallest pliers, she was just about to close the metal circle around the end of the bracelet when a knock on the front door startled her. The pliers clattered to the tabletop.

She frowned as she looked at the time. Who was knocking at the front door at this time of night? Oh God, what if it was another summons from the collection agency? She'd thought the agreement she'd gotten in place regarding payment installments had gotten them off her back, but had she been mistaken?

At least Martha hadn't heard the knock on the front door: the water was currently running in the bathroom for Martha's nightly bath, loud enough that it was unlikely she'd heard anything.

When Violet heard the visitor knock a second time, the knock faster and louder, she wrenched the door open with angry words on her lips. The words died when she realized it was Ash. His face was pale, his lips thin.

"What are you doing here? Did something happen? Are you okay?" The words tumbled from her lips like one long question.

"I'm fine. Can I come in? I need to talk to you."

Violet was about to ask why he couldn't have texted or called her, but the look on his face stopped her. Something was seriously wrong here. She'd never seen Ash this out of sorts: pushing his fingers through his hair, which was already totally disheveled. He had purple bags under his eyes, so clearly he hadn't slept a wink. What had happened between Sunday, when they'd returned from the tulip fields, and now?

Violet pushed away the panic that threatened to overtake her. Memories of the phone call from the police when William had died choked her for a moment, and she had to turn away to compose herself. Trying her best to hide her shaking, she gestured for Ash to go into the living room with her.

He said, "First, I need to see something with your husband's writing on it. Something you know he wrote himself."

Violet blinked. "What? Why?"

"I'll explain. I promise. But, can you just get something?"

Totally flummoxed, she went to her bedroom to dig

around in her drawer for a Valentine's Day card that William had given to her a year before he'd died. She returned to the living room and handed it to Ash.

Ash then pulled out what looked like a book of old checks. Crouching down, he opened the card and then folded the checkbook over until one of the carbon copies was visible. Violet didn't ask questions. Based on Ash's face, he wouldn't answer them anyway.

The silence was deafening. It pulled at Violet until she had to sit down to keep from collapsing from the anxiety. Her palms sweaty, she tried not to stare at the clock, but suddenly it was like the ticking got louder and louder with each passing second. *What is taking so long?*

Ash moved so he sat next to her. He pointed at the *s* in Valentines that William had written on the card. *Happy Valentines Day, Vi. Love you.* He'd never included the apostrophe in Valentine's Day, and seeing that tiny reminder of him made her swallow a sudden lump in her throat.

"Do you see the *s* here?" Ash said, tapping the card. "It's a cursive *s*."

"So?" She peered more closely. "Are you saying that's not William's handwriting?"

"No, what I'm saying is that *this* is his handwriting on these checks. The checks that are signed in your name." He pushed the checkbook toward her.

It was like her vision had to clear before she could even see what Ash was talking about. Her attention was snagged on the cursive *s* in *Eastern* written on the check. In the bottom right-hand corner, she saw her signature—

except it wasn't her signature. She'd never signed this check.

Her mouth went dry. "I don't understand," she said hoarsely. "What is this?"

"Violet, I think it wasn't one of your bookkeepers who stole from you. It was William."

Violet stared at the carbon-copy check until it felt like it was inscribed upon her eyeballs. Her breath came faster and faster, but it was like she was listening to someone else struggle to breathe from very far away.

Ash took her hand. "Violet, baby, breathe. Take a deep breath for me." Ash rubbed her back as he squeezed her hand. "Then let it out. Slowly. Now do it again for me. Deep breath in, then a deep breath out."

She focused on the feeling of his hand rubbing her back, the motion a gentle circle. She felt weirdly disembodied in that moment. It was only Ash's soft voice that kept her from floating away completely.

It was William. It was William. It was William. She wished she could say, *I knew it all along.* Or, *I'm not surprised.*

She wished rather fervently that she wasn't that much of a fool. That she hadn't been duped so easily. William, her husband, the love of her life, had betrayed her. How had he done it without her noticing?

"Do you know why he stole the money?" Her voice came from far away.

"I don't. Not yet. He also took out credit cards in your name; that's what the money was being funneled toward. There are a lot of transactions on the credit card statements, but none are specific enough to trace. I'll figure it out, though. I promise you that. I won't rest until I find where William put your money, or if it can even be recovered."

That was when she started shaking. It seemed to start from her toes until it took over her entire body. She was glad she was sitting down; otherwise she was sure she would've collapsed right then. Never in her life had Violet fainted, but at that moment, she rather wished that she would. At least she could forget what she'd just heard for one blessed second.

"Violet, did you hear me? Baby, talk to me. You're scaring me."

Violet reached for Ash's hand, holding on as if her life depended on it.

"I can't think. I can't understand how I didn't know. It didn't even occur to me. He never acted like he was doing anything shady." A sob burst from her throat. "Was he having an affair? Oh God, what if he has some other family somewhere and I never knew—"

Ash enfolded her in his arms, and although she wanted to cry, her eyes were dry.

Right then, a sound came from the back of the house, and Violet remembered with a start that Martha was still here. Getting up, she looked down the hallway to see the bathroom door still shut. She breathed out a sigh of relief. The last thing she needed was Martha to hear this news about her son. She would be absolutely devastated.

Violet returned to the living room and sank back down

onto the couch. Ash shot her a look of concern and tried to take her hand again, but this time, she shook her head. She did her best to ignore the hurt that flashed in his eyes.

For so long, Violet had told herself that her marriage to William had been perfect, until she'd been selfish enough to destroy it with her ambitions. She'd wanted to start her jewelry business because she hadn't been content with a boring office job. She'd wanted more, and look what had happened. He'd gotten so frustrated with her that they'd fought bitterly. And then he'd left and had never come back.

She wished she'd never started her godforsaken business. She wished she hadn't had to prove to herself and everyone else that she was capable of doing it. What had been the point? Her husband was dead and her business was in shambles.

The guilt, though, was punctuated with bursts of hot, almost boiling anger: anger at William, who'd stolen from her without batting an eyelash. Who'd sworn to love and to cherish her no matter what, but who'd deceived her so thoroughly that she'd been blindsided by this revelation. What else had he been hiding? At this point, she almost didn't want to know.

The bathroom door opened, followed by footsteps in the hallway. Another door opened and closed.

Violet let out the breath she'd been holding.

She turned to Ash. "You should go. I need to—I don't know. I need to be alone right now."

"Are you sure? You were about to collapse on me." Ash touched her forehead, but she jerked away. His face closed.

"I'm fine," she insisted. "I mean, I'm not fine, but I'm not going to keel over. Really. You should go."

Ash rose and went to the front door, but he hesitated when he reached for the doorknob. "You'll call me if you need anything? You've gotten a huge shock tonight. I hated that I had to tell you that, but you needed to know."

Her smile was tremulous, and she could feel her bottom lip start to quiver. *I can't break down yet. I can't. Keep it together, Violet. Just a few more seconds.*

"Yes, I know, thank you. Please, just go."

He enfolded her in a tight hug that squeezed the breath from her lungs before he finally left. Violet shut the door quietly, hoping that if Martha had heard voices, she had assumed it was from the TV.

Violet returned to the living room and gathered up the Valentine's Day card and the checkbook before going to her room. She locked her bedroom door and turned on some music. She was glad, at that moment, that her bedroom didn't share a wall with Martha's bedroom.

The click of the lock, the sound of the song's chorus drifting through her room—it was if the combination unleashed the floodgates. A sob burst forth from Violet, and she fell onto her bed, crying so hard that she had to bury her face in her pillow to muffle the sound. Her sobs shook the bed. A scream built in her throat, and it took all of her self-control to swallow it.

William, what happened to us? What happened to you? *Where did everything go wrong?*

She blamed herself; she blamed him. In her bitterness and regret, she blamed Ash for looking so deeply into things that he'd unearthed skeletons that Violet rather wished had never come to light.

Why *had* Ash been so intent on this? Why had he felt so compelled to shatter the illusion that her marriage had been built on love and trust? That illusion had been what she'd held on to ever since William had died. Without it, her world crumbled.

She cried until she didn't have any tears left. She cried until her eyes burned, her head pounded, and her throat ached. Seeing the card and checkbook on the corner of her bed, she tore up both and flung the pieces across the room in a sudden burst of rage.

"Damn you, William. *Damn you.*"

Like a popped balloon, her anger diffused. She was left a shaky, teary-eyed, exhausted mess. As she lay back down on her bed, she could only see Ash's face in her mind. She saw the hurt look he'd given her, how he'd tried to comfort her. But mostly she just heard his words, over and over again, like a never-ending litany.

It was William. It was William. It was William.

Violet didn't know how long she'd fallen into a doze, but when she awoke, her music had stopped playing. She rubbed her eyes, grimacing as her hand came away with all of the smudged mascara that had melted from her eyes.

She needed to wash her face, brush her teeth, and try to go to sleep for real.

After she'd cleaned up in the bathroom, she was returning to her room when she heard what sounded like a groan. Frowning, she listened, only to hear it again.

It was coming from Martha's bedroom.

Violet pushed open Martha's door. Her bedroom was dark, with only a little light from the streetlamps outside. Violet switched on the overhead light and gasped. To her horror, Martha lay on the floor, unmoving.

"Martha! Oh my God, Martha!" Violet turned her mother-in-law over, and Martha's eyelids fluttered, but she was clearly out cold. She let out a low moan, and the sound was the sweetest sound Violet had ever heard.

Violet's hands shook. It was like everything had come to a standstill. Finally, her brain—slow and confused—registered that she needed to call 911. Sprinting to her room, Violet grabbed her phone and prayed that help would arrive in time.

*a*sh had never driven so fast as he did after Violet called him, telling him that Martha was in the emergency room. He burst through the hospital doors and practically ran over at least one nurse to get to the front desk. He was so out of sorts that the attending nurse had to get him to take a deep breath before he could eke out the words *Martha, Fielding, where?*

"Ash!" Abby Thornton hurried up to him, which wasn't particularly fast given the size of her pregnant belly. She took his arm. "Let me take you to Violet. She said you were coming."

Ash let Abby lead him to a waiting room not far from the nurses' station. There, he found Violet slumped in a chair, her eyes closed and her face pale.

"Violet, baby." He sat down next to her and took her

hands, chafing them because they were so cold. "I'm here. It's me."

Her eyelids fluttered open. A second later, her face crumpled, and she started crying into his shoulder. Ash didn't even notice that Abby had left them alone; he didn't care about the other patients in the waiting room, although luckily, there were few.

"What happened?" Ash kept asking.

Violet shook her head and cried harder until his shirt was soaked with her tears. Finally, he snagged a box of tissues from a nearby table and handed it to her. She mopped up her face, her eyes bloodshot.

"Violet, what happened? Talk to me." When she'd called him and said something about the ER, he'd thought at first that she'd been hurt somehow. It had taken her yelling that it wasn't her, it was Martha, before the reality had registered.

"I found her in her bedroom on the floor. I thought she was dead." Violet hiccupped. "She wasn't, thank God. The doctor hasn't come to talk to me yet because they're stabilizing her, but she went into ketoacidosis." At Ash's blank look, she explained, "She's diabetic. Ketoacidosis is when you have too much sugar in your blood and not enough insulin. It's really dangerous. It can kill you, and the EMT told me if I had found her even an hour later, she wouldn't have made it."

Ash swore under his breath as he held Violet. She shook in his arms, and all he could do was rub her arms and tell her that he wasn't going to leave her for one second. He'd never seen her so unraveled. Added to that was his guilt about telling her about William just hours earlier.

She had to be absolutely exhausted. He didn't know how she was still coherent.

About an hour later, Abby returned to sit next to them. "Your mother's going to be fine," she told Violet. "It was a close call, but we were able to get insulin into her system to counteract her blood sugar."

"She's my mother-in-law," Violet whispered. Her voice was far away. "Do you know how this happened? She takes insulin, checks her blood sugar. I saw her do it earlier in the evening."

"She's not fully conscious yet, so I can't say how this happened," said Abby. "Her blood sugar was close to four hundred."

At Violet's gasp, Ash asked, "What's a normal level?"

"It depends on if you've eaten or not, but a normal rate would be between seventy and one hundred and forty. Mrs. Fielding's blood sugar level was so high that our attending physician wasn't sure if he could save her, especially given her age. She's very lucky that you called 911 when you did, Violet."

Violet sniffled. "I should've checked on her earlier. I was so caught up—" She rubbed her eyes and took a deep breath. "When can I see her?"

"When she's awake. I'll let you know." Abby touched Violet on the arm and left them.

Ash sat with Violet for a few more hours, and she dozed against him. Seeing her like this and not being able to do anything for her? He felt a piece of himself break apart. He vowed that he would do everything he could to keep Violet safe and loved for as long as he lived.

Abby finally took them to Martha's room around three in the morning. At the door, Ash said to Violet, "I don't have to come in if you don't want me to."

Violet hadn't let go of his hand. She took in a shaky breath. "No, I want you to. I don't want to be alone, although I'm sorry I've kept you up this late. I know you have work in the morning."

"It doesn't matter," he assured her. "Trent will totally understand if I don't come in."

When they entered, Martha looked absurdly small, sitting upright in the hospital bed. Wires and machines were hooked up to her, and when she saw Violet, she just said in a broken voice, "Oh, honey."

Violet tried to embrace Martha despite all the wires and IVs, letting out a watery laugh when she had to duck under Martha's IV tube to hug her.

"You scared me," said Violet. "What happened? Did you forget to take your insulin? You know I told you that I would help remind you."

Martha shook her head, effectively silencing Violet. "First," said Martha, "you should introduce me to this man standing behind you."

Startled, Violet introduced Ash to Martha, and when he shook the older woman's hand, her eyes narrowed, assessing him. He had to restrain himself from fidgeting under that eagle-eyed assessment.

What the hell does she think she can see when she looks at me? I'm not sure I want to know, he thought.

"Do you mind if Ash stays?" Violet asked Martha. "He promised he would behave."

"If he goes and gets you some coffee and something to eat first, then he can stay."

Ash murmured in Violet's ear that he'd be right back, knowing quite well that Martha wanted to talk to Violet in private. Leaving the two of them, he took the long way to the hospital cafeteria and counted down the minutes before he returned.

"You know Ash wouldn't have cared. Whatever you need to tell me, he wouldn't judge you." Violet smiled, despite the fact that her eyes hurt from crying and her head felt like it would split open at any minute. "I'll make sure you take your insulin from now on, and we'll test your blood sugar twice as often. We won't let this happen again."

"Sit down, sweetheart. I need to tell you something."

Violet sat down, her heart in her throat. Martha looked so exhausted and pale, her hair sticking up every which way. Without her usual lipstick and matching ensembles, she seemed diminished and frail. The realization that Martha wouldn't be with Violet forever made her want to start crying all over again.

"I know about everything," said Martha in a rush. At

Violet's surprise, she added, "I should've told you that I knew. I'm sorry."

"You know everything? I don't understand."

"I know that your business isn't doing well. I know you're struggling financially, and I found that summons in your bedroom a few weeks ago." Martha sighed. "Do you really think I wouldn't know? I've seen the strain on your face, Violet. I've noticed how every time I ask you what's wrong or if you're having issues with money, you never answer my question."

Guilt tore at Violet. She'd had no idea that Martha had noticed, and that only made her feel worse. She'd been so focused on her business, on money, on Ash. She'd moved to Fair Haven to take care of Martha, and within a month, Martha had almost died.

Did everything Violet touch turn to dust? Gloomy and depressed, she wondered if she was cursed.

"I'm sorry. I should've told you," said Violet. "I didn't want to worry you. I told you that I'd take care of you, and look at me. I've failed you. I'm so, so sorry." Her voice became choked.

"Honey, this wasn't your fault. It was mine. I don't want you to take that burden on yourself."

"How can I not? I should've paid more attention. I should've stayed home with you instead of going off with Ash like I was some kind of stupid teenager."

"Stop." Martha's voice was firm. "Don't do this to your-self. Sometimes things happen, and there's nothing you can do about it. Just like when William died. I know you blame yourself for his death, too."

Violet wanted to curl up into a ball and hide from the world for all eternity at the reminder of William, at the other person who she'd failed.

"That doesn't mean I won't do better," whispered Violet. "I said I'd take care of you, and I will."

Martha blew out a breath, and in that moment, Violet saw such sadness in her mother-in-law's eyes that it twisted her heart. Sadness and...guilt?

"I was stupid, sweetheart," said Martha. Violet was about to reply when Martha interjected, "No, listen to me. Let an old woman talk." Martha's lips quirked up. "Yes, I just admitted that I'm old. Not *that* old, mind you, but old enough to know that my body isn't what it used to be. I swear I'm getting wrinkles in my wrinkles."

"You look great, and you know it," assured Violet.

"And you're the sweetest." Martha patted Violet's hand. "I haven't been totally honest with you. Since before you moved here, I've been having issues with getting Harold's pension money, which I use to pay for my insulin."

"I thought insurance covered your insulin."

"It does, but not all of it. And it's gotten so expensive that I wasn't using it as often as I needed to. I knew you were struggling; I didn't want to add to your burden by telling you about my money issues. A woman has her pride, you know. I thought I could skimp on my insulin until the money came through, but I guess not. I'm just a stupid old woman, Violet. I'm so sorry to have put you through this."

Martha started to cry, and Violet's heart broke right then and there. If her guilt before had been great, now it was astronomical. She'd been so preoccupied with herself that she'd neglected the one person who should've had her full attention. She understood all too well Martha's pride, although that didn't help Violet feel any better. It only made her feel worse.

I've been so selfish. First with William, now with Martha. They both deserved better from me.

"Don't be angry with me," implored Martha when Violet hadn't yet said anything, "It was my fault completely, not yours. Don't blame yourself. Promise me?"

Violet nodded, but she knew that she was lying to herself. She would blame herself regardless.

A knock sounded on the door, and Ash entered carrying two cups of coffee and an assortment of vending machine snacks. "The cafeteria wasn't open yet," he explained as he set the items on the table next to Martha's bedside. "So I got you some Nutterbutters and Snickers. The healthiest options in there."

Seeing him smiling down at her, Violet couldn't deny the obvious now.

God, she loved him. She'd known it for ages now. She just hadn't wanted to admit it to herself. She loved him so much, but in falling in love with him, she'd neglected the person she'd sworn to take care of. How could that be a love worth pursuing?

Martha had begun to doze, and Violet gestured for Ash to follow her outside.

"Thank you, for everything," said Violet. Her voice was hoarse, and she was suddenly so tired that her knees shook. "I'm sure you're tired. You should go home and get some rest."

"Me? What about you?" He touched her cheek, and she let herself lean into the touch even when she knew she shouldn't. "You're dead on your feet."

"I am, but I don't think I can sleep. It's like I'm so tired that I can't." She let out a sad laugh. "I'm not even making sense. But you should go home. I'll head home here in a bit, if Martha is okay. I know you need to get to work soon."

"Violet, you know I'll stay with you however long you need me to."

"I know." She kissed him, as if she could wordlessly apologize for dismissing him. "But you should go," she said more firmly. "Go get some sleep."

His expression was skeptical. "Only if you promise me you'll get some sleep, too."

"I will. I promise," she lied.

Violet couldn't help but watch him walk away until he was finally out of view. Steadying herself, she returned to Martha's side, knowing full well she wasn't going home to sleep anytime soon.

17

Forty-eight hours later, Ash opened his door to find Violet standing there. She was coatless, the rain soaking her to the skin, yet nothing about her presence surprised him. He was almost relieved that she'd come to him. He ushered her inside and took her straight to his bathroom.

"You're going to die of pneumonia," he muttered.

"That's not how you get pneumonia." Her teeth were chattering so hard that Ash could barely understand her.

He stripped her of her clothes, ignoring the desire that ignited in his blood when her pale flesh was revealed. She was cold, exhausted, and grief-stricken. This wasn't the time to get hot and bothered. Pushing the lust away, he dried her off. She let him without protesting, and her lack of response was what scared him the most.

Where was the vivacious Violet he knew? This wasn't the Violet he'd fallen in love with.

He put her in one of his robes, and it was so big on her that she was swimming in the fabric. He led her to his bedroom, and she followed him like a meek child.

When he pressed a steaming mug of tea into her hand a few minutes later, he said, "Drink it. You look terrible."

"Such a flatterer," she croaked.

The jab made him smile. "That sounds more like you."

She sighed and sipped the tea. Color slowly returned to her face.

"I'm sorry," she whispered. "I just had to see you. I couldn't go home, not with Martha still in the hospital."

"How is she?"

"Better. I didn't want to leave her, but a bunch of her friends were there to keep her company. Including Dennis, her latest boyfriend." Violet's lips curled into a smile. "She said I was hovering and starting to annoy her."

"Did you get any sleep?" he asked.

"Not yet. I came straight here to see you." She set the mug down, her gaze imploring. "Can I stay here with you? I don't want to be alone."

His answer was immediate. "Of course." He kissed her temple, her hair tickling his lips. "You can stay as long as you like."

Her eyelids started fluttering only moments later, and Ash pulled the covers down from his bed. She sank down, and right as her head hit the pillow, she was fast asleep.

Ash gazed down at her for a long time. He brushed the wet strands of her hair from her forehead as he thought.

He'd hated leaving Violet at the hospital, but he'd known she'd wanted some time alone. He understood that. He'd always retreated into himself when he was hurting. Hell, he'd basically become a one-man island after his mother had committed suicide. If he didn't let anyone else in, then they couldn't hurt him.

Then Violet had happened. She'd blown his walls to smithereens. He'd thought he was impenetrable, and look where he was now. He laughed softly. *How the mighty have fallen.* Now he understood his brother Trent. If Trent felt for Lizzie anything like Ash felt for Violet, then Ash now knew why Trent was so devoted to his wife.

Ash let himself imagine the future for once. He thought of Violet wearing an engagement ring—a ring he'd bought her. He thought of her wearing white and walking down the aisle toward him. He thought of children with her blond hair and blue eyes, how they'd be smart and saucy just like her. He wanted all of those things so powerfully that he couldn't breathe.

Leaning down, he kissed her one last time and pulled her into his arms. He couldn't sleep, though, and when he closed his eyes, all he saw was the images of a future he'd never let himself imagine before.

When Ash awoke a few hours later, it was just before dawn. Violet was gone, and he almost panicked thinking she'd left him again. Then he heard water running, and he let out a sigh of relief.

Violet returned and got back into bed with him. Resting her head on his shoulder, she said, "It was all my fault. I don't think I can ever forgive myself."

He didn't have to ask what she meant. "You can't blame yourself, baby," he said. "Martha is older. Her health isn't what it used to be, I'm sure. I'm just glad you found her in time. It could've been much worse."

"No, you don't understand."

She sighed deeply before telling Ash about how Martha had been skimping on taking her insulin because she hadn't been able to afford it in recent months. The guilt and anguish in Violet's voice made Ash hold her more tightly to him.

"I wasn't paying attention," said Violet, her voice anguished. "I was so focused on myself that the one person I vowed to care for almost died. What the hell is wrong with me?"

"Nothing is wrong with you. Violet, Martha made that choice herself. She made the choice not to tell you, and she made the choice to put her health at risk. I'm not saying I don't understand why she did it, but she's a grown woman, too."

But Violet just kept shaking her head. "It doesn't matter. I should've noticed. I should've checked how much insulin she had, when she was getting more supplies, when she was injecting it, all of it."

He rested his chin on top of her head. "You can't save people who don't want to be saved," he murmured. "Believe me, I know."

Violet didn't say anything for a long moment after that. At first, Ash thought she'd fallen asleep again, but when he caught her looking up at him, his body heated. Her eyes were dark blue pools. When she pulled him down for a kiss, he sure as hell didn't protest.

The second their lips met, it was like everything important slid back into place. Groaning, Ash turned so he could rest his elbows on the bed, caging Violet in. She touched her tongue to his bottom lip, making his cock harden against his sweatpants.

God, he wanted her. He wanted to fuck her until he forgot everything and everyone but her. He needed her like he needed air in his lungs.

"Are you sure?" he whispered. "You've been through a lot the past few days."

"Yes, I'm sure. I'm not sure about so many things, but I'm sure about you." She hitched a leg over his hip. "I want to forget. Make me forget, Ash."

He could do that. He knew how to touch a woman until she forgot her own name.

Sitting up, he untied the tie on her robe until he unveiled her bare skin. Her breasts were high, her nipples already hardened peaks. He kissed her right over her pounding heart.

Ash licked the salt from her skin. Violet sighed and ran her fingers through his hair. Taking one nipple into his mouth, he swirled his tongue around it until she whimpered.

"How do you make me feel like this?" she asked

wonderingly. Her eyes were glassy, her cheeks flushed. "It's like you take over my soul."

He kissed her then, with tongue and teeth, until he felt her moans echo throughout his body.

You took over my heart ages ago, he thought. *It's just you. Only you.*

He moved down her body, kissing and licking every bit of skin, wanting her desperate for him. He wanted to taste her on his tongue first, even though he was so hard that it was painful. He wanted this to be about her. He needed to show her how much she meant to him so she'd never try to leave.

"You're so soft, everywhere," Ash marveled. He nipped at her belly. "Your skin is like silk."

Violet just arched and whispered his name. When Ash reached her inner thighs, he stayed there for a long moment. He sucked the sensitive skin there, leaving red marks. Seeing his marks on her only ratcheted his desire even higher. God, he wanted her. He'd always want her.

He could smell her arousal, and when he pushed her legs further apart, he gazed down at her dewy center until she sobbed his name softly. She so was wet and pink, so beautiful. He closed his eyes, mostly because he wasn't sure how much more self-control he could manage.

Leaning down, Ash licked her center. Her taste burst on his tongue, and as she moaned, he went more slowly. He loved how swollen with desire she already was. She desired *him*. That thought alone made him dizzy.

Ash could feel Violet's gaze on him as he licked her,

kissed her, tasted her. Her fingers tightened in his hair with every dart of his tongue against her sensitive flesh. When he began to lick her clit, her nails dug into his scalp, urging him on.

"I'm so close," she gasped. "Don't stop. Yes, like that. Oh my God..." Her words were lost on a long moan, and when Ash sucked her clit and pressed a finger inside her tight sheath, she exploded. Wetness coated his tongue with each shiver of her orgasm, and he exulted in her release. He loved that he could make her come this hard.

Wiping his mouth on the back of his hand, he got up to grab a condom from the nightstand. Violet had curled onto her side, her skin a pretty pink from her orgasm, a light sheen of sweat making her glisten in the low light.

Before he could put on the condom, though, Violet sat up and beckoned him to stand in front of her. Her mouth was just above his cock, and she smiled up at him when she pulled his sweatpants down. Her eyes widened in surprise when she realized he wasn't wearing any boxers. He laughed softly.

His cock bobbed in front of her, and when she licked her lips, his laugh turned into a groan.

"I've been dreaming of having you in my mouth," she whispered. "Like the first time. You remember?"

"Of course I remember—Christ." He hissed in a breath as she took him into her mouth. Her wet heat made his toes curl into the carpet. "Christ, Violet, your mouth is going to kill me."

She squeezed the base of his cock and began to stroke

him, timing her strokes with the bobbing of her head as she sucked him. Her tongue swirled around the tip, and with each motion, he felt his balls draw up. God, he was already so close. If she kept this up, he'd be done before they'd even started.

Ash gathered up her hair. "Violet, I'm about to come. Do you…?"

She just hummed and quickened her rhythm. Ash let himself revel in the pleasure she gave him for a few moments, until he gently disengaged from her mouth right before his own release was about to hit him.

Shit, he thought dazedly, *I've never almost come that fast from a blowjob.*

"I want to be inside you," he said, his voice hoarse.

Grabbing the discarded condom, he slid it on and climbed onto the bed once again. Violet wrapped her arms around him as they kissed. Ash hooked her legs over his arms and slid inside her.

They both moaned as he filled her. Ash clenched fistfuls of the covers, forcing himself to be still until he could get his raging desire under control. He didn't want to come before she came again, too.

Breathing like he'd run a marathon, he began to make love to her. Her tight heat made him see stars behind his eyelids.

"Ash, Ash, Ash." Violet bucked her hips each time he thrust inside her. "Faster. Harder. I want you to fuck me."

The vulgarity on her lips only urged him on. Kissing her, he fucked her so hard that the headboard bounced against the wall. She dug her nails into his shoulders, and the bite of pain only made him go faster. He felt her reach between them until she could rub her clit in time with his thrusts.

Goddamn, she was amazing.

He felt her tighten around him right before she let out a yell.

"You coming for me, baby?" he crooned. "I can feel you. God, you're beautiful. I can't get enough of you."

Her eyes rolled back into her head as she began to come, her body shaking like a rag doll. Growling, Ash pulled out and flipped her onto her stomach before pushing back inside her. He spanked one ass cheek and then the other. Violet cried out, but he only heard pleasure in the sound.

"You're going to come one more time for me," he vowed as he pounded into her.

"No, I can't—" Her words were lost on a moan.

She pushed against him with each thrust despite her protest. He could feel her body tightening a third time. It was only a matter of minutes before her last orgasm hit her.

A muffled scream filled the room as she shook. Ash groaned and swore as he fell off the cliff, too, thrusting into her in a jerky rhythm. He couldn't get enough air into his lungs. Sweat dripped from his chin onto Violet's back.

His world went black. He roared his release, and he heard the words *God, I love you* echo in his mind.

When he opened his eyes, he realized that he'd said the

words aloud. Her eyes were wide with shock, and he had a feeling it wasn't from having three orgasms, either.

Shit. So much for keeping it to myself.

He discarded the condom in the trash can and lay down next to her. They were both breathing hard, and Ash had to let his body calm down enough for him to come up with the words to explain.

"You love me?" she whispered. "Seriously?"

He shrugged despite the tension building inside him.

"I didn't say the words to make you say them back," he said. Even as he said that, pain spiked inside him. The thought that Violet didn't feel the same was like a knife to the gut.

She stared up at him, confused and dazed, shaking her head.

"I'm sorry," was all she said.

To his surprise, she then reached up and kissed him. He tasted sadness in that kiss, and it broke something inside him. If she left him, if she never loved him—it was too unbearable to think about.

"We'll talk in the morning," he said. He threw the covers over them both and gathered her into his arms, the sound of her deep sigh a melancholy lullaby as he slid into sleep.

18

*V*iolet groaned as she awoke to the sound of someone talking. It took her a long moment to come out of her dream to realize it was the sound of Ash's voice. Opening one bleary eye, she saw him pass by his bedroom, his phone up to his ear.

"Great, that's fantastic news," she heard him say. "Yes, I'll be down there by this afternoon. Great. Thank you."

Violet yawned. She needed to get back to the hospital before Martha was checked out. Glancing at her phone, she saw that she had a little time to spare.

Her stomach rumbled ominously. When had she last eaten? She couldn't even remember.

It'd been two days since Martha had been admitted to the hospital. When Violet had left to go home to get some sleep, she hadn't intended on going to Ash's. Yet the thought of going to that house without Martha had been unbearable. Like she couldn't control herself, she'd driven straight to Ash's, not caring that it was late or that it was pouring down rain.

She'd just needed to see him. To be with him. She shivered as she remembered how he'd looked at her as he'd thrust inside her.

And had he said that he loved her? She hadn't been certain she hadn't imagined that. She'd been so exhausted and high off her orgasms that she very well could've been hearing things.

Clutching at her pillow, she tried to catch a few more minutes of sleep, but her stomach wasn't going to let her off the hook.

"Violet, are you awake?" Ash sat down on the bed next to her, and she rolled over. He was smiling from ear to ear. What news had he gotten that had made him so excited?

"I'm sort of awake." She yawned again and sat up. "I need to take a shower. Ugh. I probably smell." When her stomach rumbled, Ash raised an eyebrow.

"Let's get you something to eat first," he said. "I'm pretty sure I have at least three different kinds of cereal to choose from."

"How fancy." She slipped out of bed and found Ash's robe from the night before, knowing full well Ash watched her every move. If she weren't so exhausted and hungry, she'd pull him straight back into bed for another round of mind-blowing sex.

Ash made coffee while Violet made herself a bowl of cereal. They sat down at the dining room table, although Ash couldn't stop fidgeting. He tapped his fingers against the table, or he tapped his foot, to the point that he almost stepped on Violet's toes.

He kept smiling at her, and both exasperated and amused, she demanded, "What is it?"

"I wanted to wait to tell you, until I had signed everything, but—" He grinned, laughing a little as he leaned toward her. "Violet, you don't have to worry about your debt anymore. I took care of it. The collections agency will leave you alone from now on."

She stared at him in shock. Her tired, sluggish brain could barely comprehend what he was saying. "What do you mean, you took care of it? How?"

"When I'd figured out that William had stolen money from you—"

Violet flinched at the reminder, but Ash was too distracted to notice.

"—I knew I had to do something to help. Not just go through your books. I had savings of my own, but not enough to pay off your debt. I just got the news that the bank approved my loan to pay off *your* loan. So it's over. Everything is paid for."

Violet licked her dry lips. "How much?"

"The loan is for twenty thousand, but the interest is at a great rate. I'll be able to pay it off in no time." He took her hands, rubbing her fingers. "Violet, it's over. You're free."

It was strange, but Violet felt anything but free. She felt…hollow. She couldn't understand why Ash would do this without asking her. Twenty thousand dollars? Not to mention the ten thousand he must've pulled from his own savings. Just the thought of him spending that much money on her debt made her want to vomit.

"I can't let you do that," she finally whispered. She took her hands from his. "I can't let you spend your savings on me like that."

He frowned. "It was my decision. You were in a tough spot, and there's little chance we'll get back the money William stole from you. It was the only way."

She felt like no one was listening to her. William hadn't believed in her ability to run her own business, and now Ash thought she couldn't manage her own finances. That debt had been her burden to bear, and hers alone.

"I appreciate what you've done," said Violet, "but I can't let you pay that debt off for me. It's not right."

"How isn't it right?" Ash looked flabbergasted. "I did it because I wanted to. You needed help, and so I helped you."

It was like a wave of anger finally overtook her. She slapped her palm onto the table so hard that the dishes rattled, startling Ash.

"I didn't ask you to help me!" she cried, her face turning hot. "I didn't ask you to drain your savings, I didn't ask you to take out a loan. Ash, you didn't stop to think that maybe you should *ask* me first? That maybe I would say no?"

"I didn't have time to ask you. I just did it." His voice hardened. "I knew you would say no, but I knew that would've been a stupid decision on your part. So yeah, I did it without asking. Sue me. At least now you won't be having a collections agency coming after you over a debt you've avoided even looking at for months now."

She stared at him, incredulous. His words reminded her of William's, how he'd told her she couldn't do anything without him. She thought of how she'd argued with her husband, how he'd died when their last words to each other had been ones like these.

Everything collided until Violet couldn't breathe. She choked back a sob—whether of grief or of rage, she wasn't sure—and she got up from the table before she said something she'd truly regret.

"So that's it?" Ash demanded, following her. "You're not even going to thank me?"

Violet let out an incredulous laugh. "Thank you? You want me to thank you for going behind my back, doing this without asking me, because you think I'm so incapable of running my own life—"

"I don't think that!" he roared. She whirled to face him, her back to the wall now. "I don't think that, because I love you! I did it because I love you and I want to fucking marry you!"

They were both breathing hard at this point. Violet couldn't speak. The words she'd so longed to hear in the daylight had been said, and by the man she loved in return.

But now… now they felt tainted. She took in a shuddering breath.

"If you love someone, you don't do things like this without asking them," she whispered. "You don't go behind their back. You don't use it like a sledgehammer to bend them to your will."

"That wasn't why I did it. I did it because I love you, and I wanted to help you. It was my choice." The anger in his voice dissolved, and he touched her cheek. "Why shouldn't I do something like this for the woman I love? Violet, I love you. *You.* I never thought I'd love any woman as much as I love you. You've turned my world upside down, and Christ, I don't even care. I just want to spend the rest of my life with you."

She closed her eyes. It was strange, to think of William now, but she did. He'd said similar words to her when he'd proposed. *You're the only woman I've ever loved. Marry me, Vi.* They'd been so happy, until she'd ruined it. Until William had ruined it, too. Until Ash had pushed and pushed to show her the truth about William—and why? What was the point? William was dead. What could Violet do now that she knew of William's perfidy?

"I'll make you so happy," said Ash. "I'll show you what a real relationship, a real marriage, can be. Not like what you had." He bent down, his lips near her own. "Say yes."

She was so tempted to say yes to him that his lips touched hers in a kiss before she could find the strength to push him away. She ducked under his arm and headed to the bathroom.

Inside, she grabbed her panties and bra and decided to forgo both. Tugging on her jeans from the night before, she grimaced when she found that they were still damp. She pulled off the robe and slipped her T-shirt on, not caring that Ash watched her from the doorway. Where were her socks? Growling, she pushed past Ash and found her shoes and socks still by the front door.

"Violet—" He grabbed her arm. "Dammit, talk to me. What the hell is going on?"

"I'm leaving, that's what's going on." She swore when she realized she'd left her phone in Ash's bedroom. As he followed her from room to room, she almost laughed at this ridiculous routine of theirs.

"Goddammit, will you stop for one fucking second?" He gripped her wrist, not hard enough to hurt, but enough to keep her from leaving his bedroom. His eyes blazed. "Explain yourself."

"You really want to do this right now? Fine. Why did you feel so compelled to find out the dirty details about my dead husband?" Her voice choked on the words, tears pricking at her eyes. "Why couldn't you have left it alone?"

"What the hell are you talking about? I was trying to help you, and you needed to know the truth."

"I didn't need to know! Don't you see? He's dead, Ash. William is dead, and it's my fault. If I hadn't gotten so angry with him that night, he wouldn't have driven off and gotten hit by a car. He would still be here. If I hadn't been so dead set on this stupid, pointless business, he wouldn't have done what he had. It was my fault!" She was panting at this point, tears streaking her cheeks.

Ash's face closed. "And what about him?" he asked harshly. "He stole from you. How is that okay? He was a shitty husband to you—admit it. Anyone with two brain cells to rub together could see that."

She shook her head. "I know that William screwed up. If he were here right now, I'd tell him so. I'm not saying he deserves to be called innocent, but that doesn't mean he was the only one in the wrong. A marriage is two people. Two. And if anyone screwed up the most, it was me, because I brought him to that point." She tried to wipe the tears from her cheeks, but they just kept coming.

"And now I almost lost Martha because I was so focused on myself. She almost died, and I don't think I could've taken it if I'd lost her, too."

"What are you saying?" rasped Ash.

"I'm saying I can't keep doing this. I can't keep doing this with *you*." She swallowed, the lump in her throat growing. "I'm saying that this is over."

"You don't know what you're saying. I'm sorry about the money, but you're overreacting. I've only tried to help you. Is this how you act when people try to help you?"

"Just because your intentions were good doesn't mean you can't still hurt people. And I'm not going to keep hurting people with my own decisions if I can help it."

She stepped forward, but Ash didn't move. They gazed at each other, and Ash's Adam's apple bobbed in his throat.

Reaching up, she allowed herself one last kiss. He groaned in the back of his throat when their lips touched.

"I'm sorry," she whispered as she broke the kiss. "Don't follow me."

When Violet arrived back at the hospital, she parked her car, staring at nothing. She felt herself begin shaking, and then the tears really came, a torrent of grief. Leaning her forehead against the steering wheel, she cried until she had no more tears left.

19

*V*iolet had never understood why people hated the rain so much. She loved it. Gazing out onto the cityscape of Seattle as the rain poured down, she felt a sense of peace for the first time in weeks.

"Violet, do you want anything from the store? I thought I'd stop by after I get coffee," Vera called from the hallway.

Violet had come down to Seattle to stay with Vera and her family, mostly at Martha's insistence that Violet get away from town. Martha had regained her strength within a week after being admitted to the hospital, and by the tenth day, she'd been getting crotchety at Violet's hovering. Violet hadn't had the courage to tell her that she couldn't bear to go out into town in case she ran into Ash.

Violet swallowed against the sudden lump in her throat. "No, I'm fine," she answered. "I'll start dinner while you're gone."

Someone yelled, and then a crash followed. More than likely Ethan had decided to play soccer in the house again.

Vera and Jim owned a pretty bungalow that was over eighty years old and located just north of downtown Seattle. Violet had been given the upstairs room. She loved that the upper level had an amazing view of the skyline and the Space Needle.

She touched a raindrop falling down the glass of the window. The thought of coffee made her think of Ash, because Lord knew everything reminded her of Ash Younger.

When she saw a playground, she wanted to cry. When she went to the Seattle Aquarium with her niece and nephew, the clown fish swimming past them made her run to the restroom to pull herself together. Sometimes she thought she heard his voice or his laugh, even here in Seattle.

She'd thought that getting away from Fair Haven would help her get over him. She'd been wrong.

If Violet didn't imagine that she heard his voice, she dreamed of him. She saw him everywhere. It was like a ghost haunting her, yet she didn't have the strength to banish it. There was almost something comforting about his continued presence in her life. Because once she got over Ash and moved on, then what?

Violet sniffled. Enough standing around feeling sorry for herself. She had work to do, jewelry to finish, dinner to start.

Both Jim and Vera worked as computer programmers,

and they rarely had time to cook for their family. Violet, being self-employed and at loose ends, had volunteered to be the family cook while she stayed with them. It was the least she could do since Vera had told her she was "a huge idiot" for offering to pay for her room and board here.

"Aunt Violet, are you going to the store with Mom?" Isabella asked as Violet began prepping for dinner. "Oh wait, I guess not, if you're chopping onions."

Isabella looked exactly like Vera, while Ethan favored his father. Isabella had Vera's dark hair and shorter stature, although sometimes Violet swore that Isabella had Violet's smile. At eight years old, Isabella was at the age where Violet felt like she could have actual conversations with her niece. When she'd been a baby, Violet had always felt like she had no idea what to do with Isabella. You couldn't exactly talk about different kinds of jewelry clasps or the pros and cons of plastic versus glass beads with a toddler.

"I told Mom she should get me coffee, too, but she won't let me drink coffee," said Isabella. "I told her that my friends drink coffee all the time because we live in *Seattle*." She rolled her eyes, even as she was staring at something on the tablet Jim had given her for her birthday. "Violet, do you think I should be able to drink coffee?"

"I didn't drink coffee at your age. I didn't like it. It was too bitter."

"I like it. My favorite is a cortado. They even give you a cookie when you get one at most places."

Violet bit back a smile. She had a feeling Isabella

preferred the cookie over the strong espresso drink, but she wasn't stupid enough to say as much.

Violet began chopping carrots, letting the sound of the faint jazz music that Vera always had playing lull her until her thoughts faded away. The tactile feeling of cooking, the sound of it, the end result—all of it had been something Violet had enjoyed. She'd especially enjoyed making food for a bigger family lately.

For so long she'd just cooked for herself and William, and then just herself for a while until she'd moved in with Martha. That had been the worst, only cooking for one. It was depressing to have so many leftovers that oftentimes she didn't eat in time before they went bad.

"Aunt Violet, are you depressed?" Isabella asked suddenly. "Because my mom says you are."

Violet froze mid-chop. "Why would your mom say that?"

"I heard her say it to my dad. Last night. She says I'm not supposed to eavesdrop on people's conversations, but is it my fault that I hear things when I'm going to my room? If they wanted to keep it a secret, they shouldn't have been talking so loud."

Violet couldn't disagree with that logic.

"Anyway, I heard my mom say that you're sad all the time and she doesn't know how to help you. I didn't know that you were sad, though. You don't look sad. Are you?"

Violet swallowed. "Am I what?"

Isabella blew out an annoyed breath. "Are you sad?

Maybe you should go home. I get sad when I'm away from home for a long time."

Violet struggled to find an answer. She hated that Vera was worried about her. When Violet had called her sister to ask if she could come stay with her, Vera had said yes without asking any questions. Violet had been grateful for that. Now, two weeks later, Violet had only talked about Martha with her sister. She hadn't even alluded to Ash, because the topic was still too painful to broach. She also hadn't told her about what Ash had discovered about William. It was all too painful to discuss right now.

"I do miss home," Violet admitted as she began to chop the celery. "But I wanted to get away for a while. Besides, you like having me around, right?"

"Oh, sure, you cook way better than Mom. But I think if you're sad, then you should figure out why. When I'm sad, I like to watch my shows. Or I listen to music. I have a playlist that I made just for when I'm sad."

Violet laughed. "Do you? I'm impressed."

"I'll send it to you." Isabella picked up her tablet, and Violet was sure that her niece had sent her her playlist, and probably her top five websites to make herself feel better. Kids these days amazed her with their ease with technology.

During dinner, Violet said little. Ethan and Isabella chattered enough to fill any silence from the adults. Vera shot Violet a few concerned looks, but Violet pointedly avoided her sister's gaze. Her issues were her own problem.

Violet wasn't going to burden Vera with them when she had a family to think about.

Violet went up to her room for some alone time after dinner. She looked out the window, the night skyline twinkling with the city's lights. She couldn't help but wonder what Ash was doing right then. Had he moved on from her? Had he already found another woman to take home to his bed? The thought made her ill.

Ash had texted her multiple times after she'd left his place that morning, but she'd ignored him every time. He'd called her, too, and she'd listened to the voicemails because with Ash, she had no self-control. Even though his voice had been filled with hurt and frustration, she'd listened to those voicemails so many times she'd memorized them. She'd then forced herself to delete them and had blocked his number. After that, he hadn't attempted to contact her again through other means.

It was better this way, she reasoned. Ash had gone behind her back, taking out a loan under his own name to pay off *her* debt. She'd never asked him to do that, and she certainly never would have. She had her pride, too, and having another man think that she was incapable of managing her own affairs only fueled her anger toward not only Ash, but William, too.

She knew now that her marriage hadn't been perfect. William had made mistakes, and so had Violet. She still blamed herself for going forward with her business at a time when William was having issues with work, but sometimes in the dark of the night, she wondered if he would've still stolen from her regardless of whether or not she'd started a business. Maybe not stealing money, but stealing her time. Her confidence. Stealing the love that she'd had for him.

Violet dug her fingers into the window frame. Why had Ash been so intent on showing her the truth about William, though? Why had he needed to prove to her that her marriage had been a massive failure? Strangely enough, in that moment she was angrier with Ash for uncovering the truth than she was with William for his betrayal.

She knew that that line of thinking was absurd, nonsensical. She knew that anyone would tell her she was being grossly unfair to Ash. But her emotions were so tangled up with anger and grief that it was like she'd trapped herself inside the complicated web.

"Can I come in?" Vera knocked lightly before pushing open Violet's door. "Are you okay, Vi?"

Violet couldn't bring herself to smile. She sighed and shook her head. "I'm a hot mess. How did you know?"

"Because I'm not blind?" Vera shut the door and pointed to the bed, motioning at Violet to sit down. Vera sat down next to her. "I thought when you came here that you just needed some time, but if anything, you look worse. What happened? I know this isn't just about Martha."

Violet felt the tears coming, and she hated herself for it. She was so tired of crying. "You remember the man I met?"

"The one you had a one-night stand with? Yes, I remember."

"Our one-night stand turned into...multiple-night stands. He wanted to make things official and I did, too."

Vera frowned. "That's good, right?"

"It was." Violet sniffled. "It was really good. I fell in love with him." Her voice caught, and she had to swallow against the lump in her throat to keep the tears at bay.

"What did he do? Or is this about William? You're allowed to love again, Vi. You can't beat yourself up for moving on."

"No, I mean, I know that," said Violet with a sigh. "At least, that wasn't the main reason. Ash went behind my back and paid off my debt."

"What debt?" asked Vera in confusion.

Grimacing, Violet told her sister about the unpaid loan, the summons, the collection agencies hounding her, all of it. Vera's face turned grave.

"Why didn't you tell me?" Vera asked, hurt in her voice. "I would've helped you out."

"I couldn't have asked you that. You have your kids to think of. It was my problem to deal with."

"So I'm assuming Ash paid it off for you, and that's why you broke up."

"He did it without asking me. I never, ever hinted that I expected him to do that. He thought he knew better than I did. You know who thought the same? William. He never believed in me when I started my business. He did my books because he said I couldn't do them right." Violet was breathing hard at this point, her blood pounding in her temples. "Why can no one trust that I know what the hell I'm doing with my own life?"

Vera sighed. "I didn't know that about William, but I'm not surprised. He always seemed…"

"What?"

Vera's nose wrinkled. "Petty, I guess. He wasn't a bad man, but he seemed so immature when you married. I'd hoped that marriage would help him grow up, but it sounds like that wasn't the case."

Violet knew she needed to tell her sister about William stealing money from the business. Humiliated, she finally told Vera the entire story in a halting voice. Vera's expression shuddered, and Violet desperately wondered what her sister was thinking when she'd finished.

"So that's everything." Violet laughed, but it was hollow. "My life is a mess. My husband lied and stole from me. My now-ex-boyfriend went behind my back and paid off my debt without asking me. Oh, and my mother-in-law almost died. Great, right?"

Vera remained silent a long time before she spoke. "I wish you would've told me," she said quietly, taking Violet's hand. "All of this was such a huge burden. No one person could've taken this all on. I'm amazed that you're still standing."

Violet started crying, and she put her head on her sister's shoulder and let the tears fall. Vera soothed her like she'd done when they were kids. Violet let the sobs overtake her for a long moment. After this latest bout of tears, though, Violet felt better than she had in weeks.

"I know you're angry with Ash," said Vera, "but unlike William, he wanted to help you."

"He wanted to prove to me that William wasn't a great husband," said Violet bitterly.

"Don't shoot the messenger. Ash figured out the truth, and he told you right away. You can't judge him for that. I think you're just scared to love again, and you've decided that it's easier to avoid it altogether. If you tell yourself Ash was in the wrong just like William, then you can be alone, right?"

Violet didn't want to hear those words, but the truth of them penetrated the fog in her brain. She knew Vera was right: she'd misjudged Ash and had lashed out at him as a result. Her heart plummeted to her toes at that realization.

How can I get him back after what I've done? I wouldn't blame him if he refused to see me again.

"I agree that Ash should've asked you before paying off your debt, but men aren't great with thinking before they act." Vera's expression turned wry. "Ask me how I know."

Violet let out a watery chuckle. Impulsively, she hugged her sister hard, and Vera hugged her back just as hard.

It hurt, knowing what William had done. Violet allowed herself to feel that pain for the first time since Ash had revealed the truth to her. It also hurt to accept that her marriage hadn't been as perfect as she'd wanted it to be. In a way, Violet knew that she had to grieve the loss of that illusion like she had grieved the loss of her husband.

But once she was free of the past—of its betrayals and its heartaches—then maybe she could finally embrace her future. A future that she hoped included the man that she loved.

*a*sh didn't know what had brought him here. He never came to the cemetery, because God knew he had never missed his parents. As a child, he'd missed his mother, but as he'd grown, he'd realized he'd missed the woman she could've been—not the woman she had been. His father, for all he cared, could rot.

But come to the cemetery he had on a cloudy May afternoon a month after he'd last seen Violet. Bitterness welled up inside him just thinking of her. He'd told himself that love was bullshit, but had he listened to his own advice? No, and look where he was now. A pathetic lovesick loser who no one wanted to be around because he was so surly.

Trent had finally told him to get his act together or he could work from home until he did. In a rage, Ash had told his brother to go fuck himself and stalked out of the Fainting Goat. He'd been close to quitting completely. That was until Trent had texted him later to say, *I'm worried about you. Can we talk?*

No, he did not want to talk to his brother. Ash had ignored the message. There was nothing to talk about, anyway.

He'd told Violet he'd loved her. He'd tried to help her—hell, he *had* helped her. But she'd thrown it back in his face and had rejected him. The memory of her words, the way she'd looked at him, haunted him.

Ash squinted up at the sky. Some of the clouds had parted to reveal slices of the sky, the sun shining through, and the world seemed inordinately bright right then. He preferred the gray. It matched his mood.

Laughing under his breath, he wandered the cemetery with no destination in mind. A few people were there, some with flowers or stuffed animals, others by themselves. One woman sat on a bench in front of a gravestone, wiping her eyes every so often. Ash looked away from her. Her grief was too palpable.

He knew exactly where his parents were buried: on the edge of the cemetery, with new headstones. His mother's plot hadn't been marked for years after her death. It had only been after their father's death that Trent had paid for both headstones. Despite his antipathy toward them both, Ash had also contributed to getting their plots marked. He'd done it more for Trent than anyone else.

When Ash rounded a copse of trees that surrounded the cemetery, he stopped short when he saw someone was already at his parents' plot. Thea sat on the grass, her legs crossed, looking like some kind of wood fairy. Fresh flowers had been placed in front of each headstone. Ash watched his sister for a long moment, mostly to make certain he wasn't interrupting something.

"Do you come here often?" he asked her quietly.

She didn't turn, but she didn't seem surprised to see him, either. "Sometimes. Sometimes I just need to talk to them for a bit."

"Why?" Ash had never understood Trent or Thea's attachment to their parents.

"It's complicated." Thea plucked a piece of grass and fiddled with it, her blond hair bright in the sunshine. "I won't say that they were good parents. They weren't. But you also weren't old enough to remember them before it all went to shit. If you can believe it, there were happy times. I try to focus on those instead."

Ash snorted. "A few happy times don't make up for a lifetime of misery."

"Maybe. Maybe not. I'm not saying they didn't fuck up, because they did. But Mom was also seriously ill, and no one helped her."

Ash sat down next to his sister, sighing. "I don't blame her as much as I blame Dad," he admitted. "He was a mean asshole. We all saw how he took his anger out on Mom. It's no wonder she killed herself."

"I forgive them," said Thea. At Ash's incredulous look, she smiled, albeit sadly. "Letting what they did overshadow my life isn't worth it. Is it ever?"

Ash didn't say anything. He didn't know if he had the

strength to forgive his parents like Thea did. He admired her for it, even if he didn't agree with it.

"So that's it, then? You forgive, forget, move on?" asked Ash. "I wish it were that simple."

"I have a feeling you aren't talking about our parents anymore," she replied sagely.

Ash didn't want to talk about Violet, yet at the same time, he desperately wanted to talk about her. He hadn't told anyone what had happened between them. When Thea had tried to get him to open up right after Violet had left, he'd lashed out and told her to mind her own fucking business. She hadn't spoken to him again for a week after that.

"I was right," said Ash, his voice dull. "Love is bullshit. I don't think it even really exists. It's just something we tell ourselves when shit hits the fan. But what does it matter when the person you thought you loved doesn't even give a damn?" He almost snarled in disgust. "I knew better, but I didn't listen. I told myself that Violet was different. I told myself I could make her see, make her get over her shitty husband. I was wrong."

Thea made a noncommittal noise. Ash took that as a sign that he should continue speaking.

"I wanted to help her. She was in debt up to her eyeballs. She had no way of getting out from under it. So I applied for a business loan for the amount she owed, and I paid off her debt. She threw that in my face, said I shouldn't have gone behind her back like that." He knew he sounded like a sulky child, but at that moment, he didn't care. "I told her I loved her, too. And she left."

Thea finally turned to face him, and to his shock, she slapped him upside the head hard enough that he yelped.

"What the fuck?" he demanded. "Are you five?"

"No, but you are. At least, you're acting like you're five." Thea rolled her eyes at his affronted expression. "Love isn't bullshit, oh brother of mine. But what is bullshit is when you do something huge like that and then are surprised when said person isn't totally in love with your gesture."

"I paid off her debt! How is that not something anyone would be happy about?"

"I'm not saying Violet didn't overreact. She probably did. She has issues, just like you have issues. But you know very well that one of your faults is that you do things without thinking. You saw this as a way to help Violet. Yet how do you think it made Violet feel?"

He rubbed the back of his head, frowning. "She said it was like I didn't believe she could manage her own life."

"Oh, so she did tell you. And, what, you didn't believe her?"

"She was wrong! I don't think that at all."

Thea rolled her eyes. "Look, Ash, I love you. Even when you're an idiot—which is what you're being right now. Good intentions are lovely, but that doesn't mean the results are what you'd intended. If I accidentally step on your foot but tell you, 'oh, I didn't mean it, sorry!' it doesn't make your foot hurt less. You know what I mean?"

"No," was Ash's confused reply. "And besides, if telling a woman I love her ends with her running away to God knows where, then I've just proven what I've always said. Love is a fairy tale. Love is just used to control people, to get them to do what you want them to do. Love is why Mom stayed with Dad when he beat her up. Love is why she ended up killing herself instead of getting help, because she thought that Dad would save her." Ash spat the words, more at the headstones in front them than at Thea right then.

"Real love isn't like that," said Thea. "No, listen to me. What Mom and Dad had..." Thea shook her head, her eyes sad. "It was love in the beginning, but it got twisted. Love doesn't mean hurting someone. Love is the opposite of that. Look at Trent and Lizzie. Hell, look at any number of couples. I swear they're all falling in love around here. It's like a disease. And they're happy and totally normal. Nothing like our parents."

Ash didn't want to listen to his sister, even as his mind told him that she was right. He wanted to wallow; he wanted to keep thinking that he hadn't done anything wrong. That he hadn't fucked up his relationship with Violet because he did first, thought later.

You always push too hard. You run right over people's feelings without a second thought.

He groaned, remembering Kayla's text. He'd done the same thing to her, and he'd brushed it off. He'd thought she'd overreacted. And Kayla hadn't been a woman he'd even loved.

"Then why did Violet run away?" he asked, his voice hoarse. "Why not stay and work it out? I could've, I don't know, cancelled the loan. Something. I could've made it right."

"I would imagine that you scared the shit out of her. She lost her first husband. If you think love is bullshit, then *she's* terrified of getting hurt a second time. Come on, Ash, use your brain for once," joked Thea.

Ash's brain hurt at the moment. Thea's words washed over him like a wave that uncovered the seashells underneath the sand.

He couldn't say that she was wrong because he knew that she was right. He'd run over Violet's feelings, her needs, in an effort to prove to her that he knew better. Would he have reacted the same if she'd done that to him? Probably. They both had their pride, that was for sure.

Ash traced one of the letters on their mother's headstone. "I wasn't sad when she died," he admitted, not sure why it mattered now. "I waited to feel sad, and it never came. How fucked up is that?"

"I think you *were* sad, you just pushed that pain away. Or expended it elsewhere. Like with other women."

"Damn, Thea, when did you get so wise all of a sudden?"

"Me? I've always been wise. You just had your head too far up your ass to notice."

Laughing, Ash threw his arm around his sister and gave her a bear hug that soon had her struggling to free herself.

"Any tips on how I can get Violet back?" he asked as Thea stood.

"Apologize. Grovel. Make things right. Don't let her run away again."

"I figured as much," he said wryly.

"Then I guess you don't need my advice anymore, do you?" She smiled and ruffled his hair. "See you later, little brother. Don't do anything I wouldn't do."

Ash sat at his parents' headstones as the afternoon passed. He didn't know what he wanted here—understanding? Absolution? Perhaps he simply wanted someone to tell him that everything would be all right. He touched the date of his mother's death and a lump formed in his throat.

"I wish you could've been strong enough to stay," he whispered. "I wish you had had a happier life. I'm sorry I couldn't help you."

As the wind blew through the trees, as Ash let his mind fall silent and he just listened, he felt the heaviness on his shoulders lift for the first time in forever. His heart lightened. The love he'd discovered for Violet blossomed and unfurled until he realized that love couldn't be a prison: love was what set you free.

"I hope you've found some kind of peace. Both of you." He addressed both of his parents. He didn't know if this was forgiveness, but it was, at least, moving on. He didn't want the ghosts of his past to haunt him any longer. Ghosts didn't keep your bed warm at night; ghosts couldn't love you.

He wanted life. He wanted Violet.

God, he wanted Violet.

He didn't know where she was right now, but he could go to Martha. He could beg her to tell him, even if she threatened to call the police on him. Ash had no pride at this point. If he could convince Violet that he truly loved her, that he wanted a life with her—it would be worth it. No matter the price.

21

*V*iolet stared out at the shining waters of Lake Union and wondered if William was looking down at her right now. She wished she could talk to him, to ask him about everything. She wanted to tell him that she loved him, but she hated that he'd betrayed her, too. It was a tangled web of emotions.

Today was the anniversary of his death. In lieu of a burial, William's will had requested that his ashes be laid to rest on Lake Union, which sat in the middle of Seattle.

That day when she'd had to scatter William's ashes over the water had been the hardest of Violet's life. She hadn't wanted to part with her husband's ashes at all. It had been the last part of him she had. Once they were strewn across the lake, that was it. She'd have nothing of her husband left.

The wind was cold off the water, and Violet shivered.

She wished she'd brought a hat and scarf, even in May. The clouds threatened rain, gray and stormy in the distance, yet Violet didn't mind. Standing in front of a railing, with the rolling hills and industrial remnants of Gas Works Park behind her, she tried to figure out what she wanted to do.

She wanted Ash—that she knew. She wanted his arms around her, his voice telling her everything would be all right. She wanted to feel him push her onto his bed again, feel his mouth on her own. She rather desperately wished to tell him she loved him. But how could she when she'd hurt him so badly? He could've contacted her through social media if he'd wanted to. But he hadn't tried since those first few days a month ago.

Violet sighed. If she couldn't talk to Ash, she wished she could talk to William.

I just wish I could ask you why, she thought to her husband. *Why did you steal money from me? Why didn't you just tell me you needed help?*

Violet had loved William wholeheartedly, and she chose to believe that their marriage had been good in the beginning. There had been love, trust, laughter. William had adored her, but somehow he'd decided to make one bad choice after another. Perhaps things had snowballed until he'd felt like he couldn't say anything. Maybe he'd planned on repaying her.

Maybe, maybe, maybe.

Violet's wedding ring winked on her finger. She twisted it off, and in a burst of anger, she was about to toss it into the lake. But something stopped her. Why couldn't she find the strength to finally let go?

"Vera said I'd find you here." Violet turned to see Martha walking toward her, a sad smile on her face. Martha's cheeks were pink, and Violet thought she'd never looked better.

"What are you doing here?" asked Violet. "When did you get in?"

"What do you think I'm doing here? I'm saying hello to my son."

Violet fell silent. She hadn't told Martha about William's theft, and she hadn't planned ever to tell her. It would break Martha's heart. She'd adored her son and had thought he'd hung the stars in the sky. As her only child, he'd been Martha's world. Her devastation at his death had matched only Violet's.

"You know I love you, Violet," began Martha. A wry smile touched her lips. "But you're the most stubborn person I've ever met besides my son. Sometimes I'd like to shake you until your teeth rattle."

Violet blinked. "What?"

"Sweetheart, I heard everything. When your man— Ash, right?—stopped by the house. I heard him talking about what William had done. The money, all of it."

Violet stilled, shock pulsing through her. Why hadn't Martha said anything?

"Oh God, is that why you collapsed?" Violet clutched at the railing. "I thought you were in your bedroom. I didn't think you could hear—"

Martha shushed her. "I heard enough. And, no, that didn't cause me to go into ketoacidosis. Not taking my insulin was the culprit there." Her voice was so dry that Violet had to stifle a laugh.

"Okay, but then why didn't you mention it? It had to have been a shock."

Martha let out a sigh. "It was, and yet it wasn't. Let me tell you something, my dear: my son was the love of my life. But I knew that because he'd been an only child, I'd spoiled him rotten. I'd believed for so long I couldn't have children, and then he came, my miracle baby. He'd always gotten his own way because of that. When things were good, it didn't matter. He was happy. But when things didn't go how he wanted them to go, well, he'd revert to the child I knew."

Violet frowned. "Immaturity is one thing; stealing is another."

"Of course, but I don't think you knew that he was about to be laid off, did you?" At Violet's wide eyes, Martha nodded. "I thought as much. You knew that his company kept moving him from job to job, of course. It got to the point that he was going to be laid off, too. He called me one night, terrified. If he lost his job, you two would lose your house. The car. Everything. The economy was so bad that he didn't know how he'd get another job that paid as much as his old one."

Violet digested this information, the puzzle pieces slowly clicking together. She'd known that William had been stressed over his job, but he'd never told her the extent of it.

"I don't know this for certain," said Martha, "but I have a feeling William was taking money from you to pay your bills, along with fancier things. Like that vacation you two went on in Miami. Things like that. He didn't want to let on how bad things were."

"Why didn't he just tell me? Or ask? I don't get it. I wouldn't have told him no. He was my husband."

Martha sighed. "I agree, and I would've told him as much. But pride has a way of making us do stupid things. He probably didn't want to worry you, either."

Right then, Violet wished she could shake her former husband until *his* teeth rattled. Everything Martha was saying made sense. The only consolation was that William had stolen money to take care of *her*, instead of using it on God knows what.

Stealing my *money to pay for* my *things. Oh, William, you idiot.*

"Like I said: he was childish," said Martha. "I knew that when you married him. I'd hoped that marriage would make him less childish, and I think it would have. Eventually."

After a beat of silence, Martha added, "He loved you, Violet. I know he did. He showed it in a stupid way, but he wanted to be a good husband to you."

"I know he did." Gazing out onto the water, Violet let the anger, the bitterness, all of it, fade away. She let it go like she'd scattered William's ashes two years ago. "I forgive him. Because if I don't, I can never move forward."

"I forgive him, too." Martha's lips quirked upward. "I also wanted to tell you that your young man came by yesterday. He wanted to talk to you. I told him I had to ask you first."

Violet's breath caught. "Ash came to see you? How did he look? What did he say?"

"He looked terrible, although still handsome, of course. He was none too happy with me when I told him that I wasn't going to tell him where you were. If I weren't an old lady, he probably would've decked me."

Violet trembled. She couldn't believe it: Ash wanted to see her. Was it because he still loved her, or did he just want to tell her how much she'd hurt him?

"What if things go south like my first marriage?" whispered Violet. "I don't think I could bear it."

"Why should it? Ash isn't William. He loves you, my dear. Don't let the past hold you back. It's never worth it."

Violet let excitement bubble inside her for the first time in a while. Ash hadn't forgotten about her. Not only that, but he wanted to see her. *Does he still love me?* It was a thought she hadn't let herself consider. She wouldn't blame him if he'd moved on, but if he hadn't? If there was even a slight chance…

"I love him," blurted Violet. "I love him so much that it hurts. I just don't know how I can get him back. I was awful to him. I pushed him away."

"Honey, that young man is completely in love with you. I saw it on his face when he was at the hospital with you. No man shows up in the middle of the night for a woman he doesn't care about. Believe me. He looked like he'd move heaven and earth just to make you happy."

"That was before, though." Violet explained to Martha about Ash taking out a loan to pay off her debt and how angry she had been. "I threw it back into his face. He told me he loved me, and I didn't say it back. It was terrible."

Martha clucked her tongue. "Sounds like you both have some explaining and apologizing to do. You're both stubborn and have way too much pride between the two of you, but that's what'll keep things interesting. God knows Harold and I had enough spats and arguments to last a lifetime, but we loved each other. That was all that mattered."

Suddenly, Violet wondered why the hell she was still standing here. She needed to find Ash; she needed to explain, tell him that she was an idiot. That she loved him. God, how she loved him. When she'd seen him at his niece's birthday party, she'd known right then that he was something special. But she'd been too heartsore and scared to admit it.

Violet's wedding ring seemed to glare up at her, mocking her. Before she could think about it, she plucked the ring off her finger and tossed it into the lake. It landed in the water with a satisfying plunk.

And in that moment, Violet was freed of the past.

"Well, that was unexpected," said Martha.

Violet laughed, tilting her head up. "I loved you, William," she said into the sky. "A part of me will always love you, but I want to move on with my life."

Martha added, "I miss you, son, every day. I'm angry with you, too, but I'll get over it. I can't wait to see you again and give you a stern talking-to." She dabbed at her eyes, sniffling.

Violet and Martha stayed until Violet was pretty sure her nose was going to fall off from the cold. Martha told her that she was staying at a friend's house for a couple of days, and so they parted ways when they returned to their cars, hugging and crying only a little.

Her heart light, Violet drove straight to Vera's and began to pack. When Vera saw Violet pulling her suitcase from the closet, she just hugged Violet and told her good luck.

"He's a lucky man. And if he hurts you, I'll kill him," said Vera.

Violet laughed, zipped up her suitcase, and headed back to Fair Haven—and to Ash.

$\mathcal{A}$sh slammed his fist against the wall of his apartment, the sound ridiculously satisfying. After three days of trying to discover where Violet had gone, he'd gotten nothing. Nothing! He'd gone to Martha's, only to have the woman basically kick him out of her house.

"If she doesn't want you to know, then I'm not going to tell you," Martha had said. "It's as simple as that."

Ash had cajoled; he'd begged; he'd been close to threatening a woman when Martha had looked at him like the lowliest of worms. He'd left, tail between his legs, cursing everyone and everything.

Violet had a sister in Seattle, but what good was that information? He couldn't very well go down to the city and knock on the door of every apartment, house, condo, or yacht he encountered. No matter how much he was tempted to do just that.

"Goddammit, Violet," he muttered, rubbing his aching knuckles. "Where the hell did you go?"

She'd still had his number blocked, his calls going to voicemail and his texts unanswered.

Ash realized that there could very well be a good reason why he couldn't get a hold of Violet: she just didn't want to see him again.

His gut twisted. If he'd truly fucked everything up, if he'd lost the one woman he'd ever loved, he'd never forgive himself. He didn't even need her to forgive him: he just wanted to apologize, to explain. To tell her that he loved her one last time.

Growling, he grabbed his keys and headed out for a walk. He couldn't stay in his apartment for one second longer, mostly because it just reminded him of Violet. He remembered how he'd kissed her right inside his front door that first time, how he'd led her to his bedroom. How she'd looked in his oversized robe, her blond hair falling down to her shoulders.

Ash didn't have a destination in mind. Since it was Saturday, he didn't need to go into work, not to mention he didn't need Trent hovering. He considered going over to Thea's but then dismissed the idea. He didn't want any of his siblings asking him questions right now. He wasn't in the mood.

When he arrived at the playground, he wasn't surprised. He laughed softly, remembering how he and Violet had swung on the swings that night. Had it really only been less than two months ago? It didn't seem possible. It seemed like a lifetime ago.

The day was overcast but warm, and the playground was filled with parents and children. Kids screamed as they went down the slides, while another group played tag on the grass. All of the swings were occupied, and Ash watched the kids swing back and forth until the image was practically imprinted onto his eyelids.

He sat down on a bench and watched the kids playing. It was inevitable that his mind strayed to thoughts of his own possible children someday. He swallowed against the lump in his throat. Violet would make an amazing mother. Would their kids be more blond like her or more redheaded like him? Would they be good with numbers or better with intricate tasks like jewelry-making? One thing he did know was that any children they might have would be a handful. Two stubborn parents together equaled kids that would probably terrify anyone else.

"Ash? Is that you?"

Ash looked up to see a woman with short dark hair approaching him. It took him a moment to recognize his ex-girlfriend Kayla. She'd cut her hair since last he'd seen her, not to mention she had a little boy with her who was probably no more than five or six years old.

"Kayla, hi," he said. He stood and held out his hand to the boy. "What's your name?" he asked the boy.

"Ash, this is my nephew, Adam," said Kayla.

Adam narrowed his eyes, like he could see into Ash's soul, before extending his small hand. Ash shook it and had to work hard to restrain a chuckle.

"Adam, why don't you go play while I talk with Ash?" Kayla suggested, and without any protest, Adam ran onto the playground and quickly joined a group of kids making sandcastles nearby.

"It's been a while," she said. "How are you?"

Ash was surprised she even wanted to speak to him. They hadn't exactly parted on great terms. She'd been so hurt when he'd tried to make decisions for her, not to mention those texts she'd sent him. He grimaced inwardly.

"I'm fine. You?" he said.

Kayla smiled. "I'm good. I'm glad I ran into you. I wanted to apologize for what I texted you. You were right: I did need to get things together. You got me that job and a place to live, but at the time, I didn't want to hear it."

"I should've asked you first," he admitted. "I realize that now. You had every right to be upset. Just because I might have been correct doesn't mean I couldn't have gone about it differently."

"Oh, I agree." At his laugh, Kayla added, "You can be…a lot sometimes." Her eyes sparkled, and Ash wasn't stupid enough not to see the interest in her eyes.

They talked for a little while longer before Adam came back, telling his aunt that he was hungry. Kayla stood on her tiptoes and gave Ash a kiss on the cheek as she departed, and he couldn't help but give her a brief hug.

As he waved goodbye to Kayla, he heard someone take in a choked breath behind him. Turning, his eyes widened.

It was Violet. And she'd just seen him embracing another woman.

VIOLET FROZE, her excitement fading to horror in a moment's time. Ash looked just as startled, and they stared at each other like two deer in headlights for what felt like an eternity.

I told myself he probably had moved on. I can't blame him if he did.

You don't know the whole story. Don't jump to conclusions.

I think I'm going to vomit.

Suddenly it felt like everyone was staring at her, mocking her, telling her what a fool she had been to think that he'd loved her enough to want her back after what she'd done. Martha had been mistaken. Ash probably had wanted to talk to her so he could tell her that he'd somehow reversed the loan. Or he wanted to tell her how angry he was with her. Not that he still loved her.

"Um, I'm sorry," she whispered, her face on fire. "I should go. I should definitely go."

She was about to turn to go when Ash caught her by her arm. She blinked up at him.

"Don't," he urged. "It's not what you think. At all. We're just friends."

Violet almost didn't hear Ash through the pounding of her heart. *Friends. Friends. Friends.*

"Friends that kiss you on the cheek?" she asked.

Ash growled. "She's my ex-girlfriend. We haven't seen each other in ages." He grasped Violet by her upper arms, his gaze steely. "She's nothing. Violet, I've missed you so much. You—you are *everything*."

At that, Violet started giggling. Not because any of this was funny, precisely, but because she'd gone from elated to horrified to elated all in the space of five minutes, and really, the only reaction one could have was laughter. It was better than sobbing, she thought, even though her eyes did tear up as she laughed.

Ash, clearly confused, let her laugh for a little while longer until he said, "Did I miss something?"

"No, no, I'm sorry." Violet wiped her eyes. "Just seeing you with that woman, I thought the worst. I thought you'd forgotten about me, and I couldn't blame you if you had. Ash, I'm so, so sorry. I was stupid. I was an asshole to you, and if you can't forgive me, I won't be upset. I mean, I will, but I won't be upset with *you*—"

He squeezed her lips shut with his index finger and thumb, just like he had when they'd first met. His confused expression had transformed into a dazzling smile. Violet practically melted from its radiance.

"You're sorry?" he repeated. "How sorry?"

"Sorrier than I can ever say." Reaching inside her purse, she pulled out a piece of paper. "I have someone willing to buy the business. I'm going to let it go. It's not worth it. I keep hurting people with it; it just drives a wedge between us."

Ash took the paper, scanning it before crumpling it in his fist. Violet blinked in surprise.

"I'm not going to let you give up on what you love," he vowed.

Now it was her turn to smile. "Don't you see, though? You're the one that I love. Not my business, not my pride— you. I love you, Ash."

The paper fluttered to the ground, and Ash stared at her until she felt his gaze like a brand on her skin.

"Say it again," he growled.

"I love you."

"One more time."

She laughed. "I. Love. You."

The ferocity in his eyes melted instantly, and right then, Violet saw how much he loved her. Wrapping her in his arms, he muttered, "Thank God."

Then he was kissing her, kissing her with such heat and tenderness that it was a marvel that she didn't melt into a puddle at his feet. He groaned, deepening the kiss. Until someone cleared their throat behind them.

"Um, there are kids here," a woman said. "Can you not do that here?"

Violet started giggling when she realized that practically the entire playground was staring at them. Some of the kids were making gagging noises, while others simply looked on in wonder. The parents, however, looked like they'd like to put them both in timeout.

"Come on, let's get out of here before we get arrested," said Violet.

Ash took her hand wordlessly, taking her into a copse of trees that surrounded the park. Twigs and leaves crunched under their shoes, and before Violet knew it, they were in a little forest, away from the world completely.

"God, Violet, I've been trying to find you for days now," said Ash, his voice anguished. "I went to Martha, but she wouldn't tell me a damn thing. Cruel woman, your mother-in-law. You wouldn't answer my calls or texts."

Violet squeezed his hand. "I know. I'm sorry. I thought a clean break was the best for both of us, but I was wrong. Completely wrong. When Martha told me that you'd been looking for me, I knew I had to come back to find you. Even just to say how sorry I am."

"*You're* sorry?" he said incredulously. "I'm the one who should be apologizing. I went behind your back and did something monumental without even asking you. You had every right to be pissed. I wanted to help you, but I know now that helping people doesn't mean running over them, either." His lips quirked. "Believe it or not, that woman you saw me with was one of the people who told me as much."

"Really?" Violet looked over her shoulder. "I should go find her and give her a medal."

"Seriously, though. Violet, I love you." His eyes blazed as he said the words, and Violet could barely catch her breath. "I never thought love was possible for me. I thought it was a fairy tale, some bullshit people made up to make themselves feel better. But with you—" He touched her cheek, his touch gentle. "With you, I know that what I believed was the bullshit. With you, I know that love not only exists, but it's exactly what I feel for you."

She laid her hand over his, tears pricking her eyes. "I

didn't think I'd ever love again," she admitted. "But you showed me that that wasn't true." Holding up her left hand, she showed him her bare ring finger. "I had to let go of some things—of some people—first. My past was holding me back from embracing my future."

Ash took her left hand and kissed where her wedding ring had once sat. "I didn't want you to forget your first husband. I know how much you loved him."

"I know. I didn't do it for you. I did it for me. It's not that I've stopped loving William. It's that I've put that love away so I can look forward to a new love." Violet wrapped her arms around Ash's neck. "I want to be with you. No matter what."

Groaning, he took her mouth. She groaned at his heat, at the way his beard scraped her chin. They were messy and wild, and soon they were grabbing at each other's clothes and pulling and tearing at them. One moment Violet was yanking Ash's shirt over his head, the next he was pushing her blouse up and kissing her breasts.

Ash sucked a nipple through the lace of her bra before blowing on the turgid peak. The cool air made her moan. Her toes curled.

"I want you," she whispered as she attacked the zipper on his jeans. She cupped him through the fabric, which made him shudder. He was already hard, and it only heightened her need further.

Ash suckled on her neck. "I don't have a condom. We can't—"

"Don't care. I'll take my chances."

Ash stilled, and when his gaze met hers, she saw need, fire. Love. "Are you sure?"

"Totally sure. Now, are you going to take off your pants or am I going to have to do it for you?"

It took all of ten seconds before Violet's back was against a tree and her legs were around Ash's hips. In one swift movement, he thrust inside her.

"Oh my God, oh my God," was all she could say as he pounded into her. The tree shook with each of his thrusts, leaves falling around them.

"I love you. I love you." He punctuated the words with the movement of his hips, and Violet felt her orgasm building with stunning speed. Reaching up, she kissed him, loving how he filled her sex and her mouth at the same time.

"I love you," she gasped. "Shit, I'm going to—" Her orgasm burst upon her and she screamed, her neck arching.

She heard Ash swear, his fingers digging into her ass, before he stilled, shouting his release. Violet had the vague thought that they'd probably been loud enough that people nearby could hear them, but she didn't have the energy to care. Her arms and legs wrapped around Ash, Violet was the happiest she'd ever been.

"Say it again," said Ash as they hastily got dressed some time later.

"How many times do I need to say it?" Grasping the front of his shirt in a fist, she brought his head down so she could whisper the words against his lips. "I love you. I love you. I love you."

"I love you, too," he said, his eyes sparkling. "And now I'm going to take you back home and show you just how much I mean it."

*V*iolet had hoped that her exhibit at the convention would do well today, but she hadn't expected this level of interest.

Then again, it helped that her boyfriend had consented to be her jewelry model this afternoon. At the moment, Ash was wearing five bracelets, three necklaces, and four rings. Earrings, unfortunately, weren't possible since he didn't have pierced ears.

He looked over his shoulder and mouthed the words *Help me* when a particularly handsy woman started handling one of the necklaces hanging from him while her other hand was caressing his bicep.

"May I help you find something?" asked Violet, startling the woman so much that she jumped. "Or have you found what you were looking for?"

Sensing that Violet wasn't playing around, the woman

sniffed and moved away from Ash with a sour look on her face.

"God, you're sexy when you're riled," Ash growled in Violet's ear.

He palmed her ass as he said the words. Violet smacked his hand away, but it was halfhearted. She touched him in inappropriate places at inappropriate venues as often as he did it to her.

"I thought you needed saving," she replied primly. Turning, she straightened the necklace made of blue and violet beads hanging from his neck that the woman had been handling. "You look so dashing in your jewelry, I have to say."

"Don't forget the deal we made." His teeth flashed white. "I get to do whatever I want to you tonight. *Anything.*"

Violet shivered and scampered back to her table, where multiple people had congregated.

Six months after she and Ash had gotten back together, she'd worked her ass off to get her business out of the red. With Ash's help and encouragement and a lot of wine, Violet had started making headway. She'd also agreed to let Ash pay off her debt—except she would then pay *him* back. Ash had protested initially, but Violet could be just as stubborn as he could. He'd finally agreed after some late-night persuasion.

To mark six months together, Ash had surprised her not with an engagement ring, but with a betta fish. The purple-red fish had darted around in its bowl, bashing into the glass when it had noticed Violet's finger on it.

"I wanted to get you that clown fish," Ash had said, "but you have to get a whole aquarium for it. Plus, they're saltwater fish, and you need an anemone or two to go with it. So, a betta fish."

Violet had fallen for her betta fish, Marty, almost as fast as she'd fallen for the wonderful man who'd given her the fish in question.

Now, at a huge convention for all kinds of arts and crafts businesses—from basket weaving to jewelry to knitwear to leather working—Violet couldn't believe how much business she had already gotten. She'd already sold enough pieces to pay for the registration fee and for all of her brochures and business cards that she'd brought with her. She just hoped that she'd brought enough to last the entire day.

Ash laughed, and Violet couldn't stop the smile from spreading across her face as she watched him interact with his newest fans. She'd never thought she could be as happy as she was now, and every day, Ash showed her how much he loved her.

Although Violet continued to live with Martha for the time being to help her keep her diabetes in check, she saw Ash as often as they both could with their work schedules. If they weren't together physically, they were texting and calling each other constantly.

"This is quite a nice collection," a woman said as she held up one of Violet's necklaces. With her silver hair in a stylish bob, lips a crimson red, the woman looked like she could be thirty or sixty.

"You make these all yourself?" the woman asked.

"Yes, I do. I also do custom designs. Anything you'd like to try on?"

The woman shook her head, although she continued to look at each piece on Violet's table with an attentive air. "I'm just perusing for now. I'm Georgia Kelson, by the way."

Violet introduced herself to Georgia, the two women shaking hands. After Violet had given Georgia one each of her brochures and business cards, Georgia wandered away from her table. Violet frowned at her retreating figure. Why did that name ring a bell?

"Hey, I'm out of rings," said Ash, displaying his bare fingers. "Got any more for me to wear?"

"Of course I do." Grinning, Violet placed the biggest rings in her stock on Ash's hands, although she had to put them both on his pinkies since they were way too small for the rest of his fingers.

"Thank you." Turning, he flashed his sparkling hands at his current groupies, wiggling his fingers. "Who wants to try on a giant ring with a dragonfly on it?" he asked in a theatrical voice.

Violet was definitely going to pay for this later that night, and she couldn't wait.

As the convention drew to a close, Violet began packing up, Ash placing the remaining jewelry in individual plastic bags. Who would've thought that he'd make the perfect jewelry assistant? Violet would never have broken up with him had she known he'd be so helpful, she thought with a grin.

"Oh, excellent, I'm glad you haven't left yet," said Georgia as she returned to survey Violet's mostly bare table. "Do you have a moment? I wanted to speak with you about a business opportunity."

Ash raised his eyebrows at Violet, and Violet shrugged, wordlessly replying, *I have no idea.*

"I actually wasn't planning on making any offers today," said Georgia as Violet followed her to a more private corner, "but I have to say, your jewelry is some of the best I've seen in a long time. And the fact that it's handmade? Fantastic."

Violet blinked. "Thank you," she stammered. "That's very kind of you."

"I'm an investor, and I'm always on the lookout for new and upcoming businesses like yours."

Georgia pulled out a card, handing it to Violet. On the back was a list of companies that Georgia had invested in. Violet's eyebrows shot up as she read the list.

Georgia Kelson…Georgia Kelson…oh my God, I know who she is! She's a billionaire! thought Violet as she barely restrained incredulous laughter.

Georgia smiled when she saw that Violet had finally recognized her.

"I want to invest in your business, Ms. Fielding," she said. "I've yet to invest in jewelry, but I have my fingers in a number of related companies. Purses, hats, scarves. How much is your business currently worth?"

Violet floundered. Her business was such small potatoes that she'd never considered that anyone would want to invest in it. She had no idea how that even worked. Shaking her head, she said, "Ms. Kelson, I'm beyond flattered, but it's just me. I don't have any employees or a storefront. I'm not sure it would be worth your while."

"Believe me, I know when something is worthwhile, and your business is." Georgia winked. Taking the card she'd just handed Violet, she scribbled something on the front and handed it back to her. "That's my offer. If you would like to discuss further, give me a call." As she was about to leave, she added, "And I have to say, your male model is darling. I hope I'll see him again if you decide to move forward."

Violet returned to Ash, flabbergasted. He shot her a concerned look.

"Everything okay?" he asked. He pointed at the card in her hand. "What was that about?"

Violet glanced at the card, her gaze landing on the scribbled number on the front. Her eyes bulged when she read the number: $500,000. She looked more closely, sure that she'd misread. Georgia must've meant to write $50,000. More likely, $5,000. But half a million? There was no way...

"Ash, what does this say?" Violet handed him the card, pointing to the amount written on it.

"Looks like five hundred thousand dollars. Why?"

Violet swallowed, her throat dry. "That woman just offered me that much money to invest in my business."

"*What?*"

"I can't believe this. Oh my God." The realization that her business could not only be saved, but could become bigger than she'd ever imagined? Violet started laughing. "Ash, do you know what this means?"

"That either this woman is crazy or you're going to be very rich?"

"Yes!" Violet snatched the card back.

She was going to frame this card. Whirling, she looked for Georgia in the crowd to really thank her, but Georgia had already left. Violet would just have to call her, wouldn't she?

"Oh, Ash, this is so amazing. I can't believe it." Violet wiped away tears of joy. "Can you believe it?"

Ash embraced her, his smile wide. "I believe it, because you're amazing. And this business is going to be amazing, and our life together is going to be amazing. Amazing, amazing, amazing. That's the only word I know."

"Actually, I don't think that's true."

He raised an eyebrow. "Really? You don't think it'll be amazing?"

"Our life isn't going to just be amazing together: it's going to be fan-fucking-tastic."

Laughing, Ash picked her up and began to twirl her around in a circle, the remaining convention-goers looking on with a mixture of confusion and envy at such obvious happiness.

THEA YOUNGER UNCAPPED her marker and began to fill in the final panel in her graphic novel. It had taken her over a year to finish this bad boy, and as she inked the character's cape with her blue marker, her sense of accomplishment only grew.

"There," she said as she finished. "It's done." Getting up, she did a happy dance in the middle of her living room, not caring in the least that there was no music playing or that if anyone saw her, they'd think she was crazy.

Thea was used to people thinking she was crazy, or at the very least, odd. She'd gotten her first tattoo at thirteen (a friend of a friend of a friend had unwisely agreed to do it). Thea couldn't regret the ugly little beetle that was still inked on her right wrist. You couldn't tell that it was a beetle at this point—it looked more like a blob with skinny arms—but Thea didn't care.

Thea didn't much care what anyone thought about her. She hadn't for a long time. She was a free spirit, she was a girl moving against the current, she was—

Oh, who was she kidding? She was a receptionist at a law office and a wannabe graphic novel artist. Except that she hadn't yet gotten the courage to actually show her graphic novels to anyone. Not even her siblings. Not even Ash, her favorite brother. She was in the small town of Fair Haven without any prospects of getting out. She'd lived her entire life here and had seen only a few bordering states.

She'd never been to New York City, or Minneapolis, and definitely not London or Paris or Rome.

Her phone rang. Answering it, she said, "What's up?"

"There's a protest on Saturday. You're going, right?" her friend Mittens Haverford III said.

Mittens's real name was Milton, but when he'd told Thea as much, she'd instantly decided to call him Mittens instead. That had been ten years ago. Now most everyone called him Mittens and he didn't have the energy to correct them anymore.

Thea had also become a vegan within the last two years and, in the process, had become an ardent animal rights activist along with Mittens. She'd always been an animal lover, although at the moment, her apartment didn't allow so much as a fish. Someday she hoped to get a dog.

It helped, too, that her current friend group was also into protesting, although initially, most of them preferred to protest things like a fountain being shut off in one of Fair Haven's parks or the use of red light cameras at stoplights.

"I'll be there," said Thea. "What's this one for? Who's being evil?"

"Bertram, Sons, & Co. What a pretentious name. They do animal testing. It's bullshit. There's no reason for it nowadays, and the people doing it are just being assholes. I'll send you the link to RSVP."

"Thanks, Mitty, darling. You're my favorite anarchist."

Mittens sent over the invite, and Thea found herself googling Bertram, Sons, & Co. out of sheer boredom. Or sheer curiosity. Those two things tended to meld together for Thea more often than not.

She discovered that the company was worth billions (no surprise), and that it manufactured cosmetics and household products. A number of the products listed were ones that Thea herself had used to use before she'd gotten involved in animal rights. Now she made certain that all of her products—from her shampoo to her dish soap—were cruelty-free, organic, palm-oil-free, and without any harsh detergents.

Clicking further on the company's website, she landed on the *About* section. At the top was a photo of a man who couldn't have been older than thirty-five: with his dark hair and equally dark eyes, he looked like something out of a Brontë novel. His gaze penetrated the screen, making Thea shiver despite herself. That gaze could put holes in you, like laser beams.

To make matters worse, Anthony Bertram, CEO, was undeniably handsome. He had a strong jaw, sharp cheekbones, and surprisingly plush lips. Thea leaned closer to the computer screen. Weren't CEOs supposed to be scrawny, pale technology geeks with no social skills?

Thea found herself searching for images of this Anthony Bertram, and when she landed on one of him at the beach, his chiseled physique on display, she fanned herself. "Hot damn, you're a sexy one, aren't you? Too bad you're evil."

She allowed herself to look at a few more photos—one was of him in a tuxedo at some fancy party, another was of him on his yacht—before she finally shut her laptop and leaned back in her chair.

So, fancy-pants, super-sexy hot CEO Anthony Bertram was their next target? Bring it on. Thea was ready for him, no matter how good he looked without his shirt on.

Her phone rang with another notification. Thea opened the email, which read, *We have an opening at our luxury cabin deep in the Cascade Mountains. Reply ASAP to book your reservation!* She promptly began squealing.

Thea had been dying to get out of Fair Haven for some alone-time for ages, but the one place she'd been saving up for was always booked. She'd finally contacted the owner to get on the waiting list. That had been three months ago.

She sent her reply, excitement bubbling up inside her. When she received the confirmation email, she performed another happy dance. This time, she turned on her favorite music and danced across her living room floor.

After Thea made Anthony Bertram and his company wish they'd never been born, she was going on the vacation she deserved, all by herself.

She could hardly wait.

WANT MORE OF THE YOUNGERS?

Don't miss out on the next in the series!

TAKING A CHANCE ON LOVE
(Thea and Anthony's story)
Coming June 2018

❦

HERON'S LANDING

Seduce Me Sweetly

Tempt Me Tenderly

Desire Me Dearly

Adore Me Ardently

ABOUT THE AUTHOR

A coffee addict and cat lover, Iris Morland writes sexy and funny contemporary romances. If she's not reading or writing, she enjoys binging on Netflix shows and cooking something delicious.

irismorland.com

Made in the USA
Columbia, SC
08 March 2018